The
Chronicles
of
Stiltshire

Dominus subulcus meus est

Contents

"Ah, Stiltshire, blessed Stiltshire, the very microcosm of England itself. She bloometh like the dew-clad skin of a sloe that hath lain three days at the foot of a stile, as yet untrampled by the constable's wife."

Thus spake Dr Edwin Stywright, Master of St Cedd's College, in 1911. Quite what he meant by the latter allegory we shall never know, for he died twelve minutes later without uttering another word. His first comment is, however, most apposite. Stiltshire is indeed a little like England in miniature; from the high hills and windswept moorlands of the north to the rugged coves and fishing villages of Dongland in the south-west, from the gentle downs, cliff-tops and elegant resorts of the south-east to the cider orchards in the west.

There are two main ranges of hills, the North Drones and South Drones, forming a long ridge which sweeps southwards and westwards. In the middle is the curious rocky outcrop of Ryming Head and at the southern end the vast, bleak mound of Witterspool Hill. After this there are only occasional prominences like Breen Hill and Chineham Heights until one reaches the Eyt Mongs and the Greyt Mong.

The flattish central plain is rich agricultural land, broken only by the remnants of a vast primaeval broad-leaved wood in Knorrley Forest, Bayconhurst Woods and Oxbake Woods. This is pig country, for the people have been swineherds since time immemorial. The place names - Hogberrow, Bayconhurst, Gruntlington, Snoutfield - and even the surnames - Pigman, Swiller or Swillmaker and of course Stywright - reflect the county's love affair with all things porcine.

Through its midst from north to south flows the great River Stilt, emptying itself into the sea through the bulbous natural harbour of Stilhaven, opposite which lies Gryatt Island, for many generations of Stiltshire mariners the last, or if they were lucky the first, sight of their homeland. Lesser rivers meander through the land: Eyve, Crachel, Tutt, Hake, Haze, Vole and Lyder, plus the chalk streams of Prume and Pebb where trout and watercress abound. Of still waters there are few: the eponymous ponds at Eftmere and Cruftmere, the dark foreboding depths and sombre shores of Ulm Water and the part natural, part man-made Wilberton Meres.

The landscape can be dramatic, as in the craggy peaks of Slack Tor and Grittersham Fell or the cliffs and coves of Dongland (including that curious coastal rock formation known as the Devil's Buttocks where on a windy day the rocks echo with an eerie rumbling sound), but for the most part it is as gentle and unassuming as the people.

Stiltshire
Now and Then

A roughly chronological excursion through the history of the county and its people.

Pre-history and Mystery

Could we peer back through the mists of time at what is now Stiltshire, we might see the morning mist slowly clearing over a lowly clearing in a great forest. Out of the dappled woods comes a figure clad in coarse animal skins, leading a flock of plump, hairy pigs.

But this is mere conjecture. We know that the lowlands were almost entirely covered with a vast broad-leaved forest, as dense as Knorrley Forest is today, and we know that pigs have been domesticated in the area for a long time, but otherwise there is scant evidence of early civilisation. If the forest was thick and impenetrable, the hills were inhospitably bleak and bare. Such prehistoric settlements as existed were probably mostly along the Stilt valley. Signs of early human habitation are for the most part unremarkable: burial mounds, menhirs, fragments of pottery, stone axes and suchlike artefacts. But there are three sites of particular interest.

Among the county's earliest man-made structures are the mysterious stone triangles at Nether Bolsacre - 22 of them averaging about the height of a double-decker bus. 18 of these structures were arranged in a triangular formation, seven on each side, with three more forming a smaller triangle in the middle and one beyond the eastern apex of the outer triangle. Although most have long since fallen over, the five that remain standing all lean precisely 7° towards the east and detailed examination shows that the others once did likewise. Equally intriguing is the way that the sides dovetail into the bases and each other, indicative of sophisticated stone cutting techniques way beyond the expertise of primitive man. Carbon dating reveals that the stones are at least 3000 years old. But why are they there? Numerous theories have been put forward, none of them particularly persuasive, including the suggestion that the site was a launch pad for alien spacecraft (see references to Morfark elsewhere in this book). The area has long had associations with the occult and became the headquarters of the notorious Brotherhood of Bollin in Victorian times.

The second strange relic of early civilisation is Wilberton Meres. Here, ten natural ponds with underground springs which form the source of the Kibble Brook are interconnected with man-made channels and rectangular basins. Originally believed to date from Roman times, the work is now thought to be much older, possibly Bronze Age. Its purpose is a mystery. The channels cannot have been for irrigation purposes, since they only connect the ponds and all the water leaves the site by the Kibble Brook as it would naturally. The rectangular basins, though superficially resembling watercress beds, are far too deep for this purpose.

Another site of great antiquity is the Squilton Fox, a chalk figure carved into a hillside in the North Drones overlooking the village of Squilton. A crude but striking representation of a running fox with tapering muzzle, pointed ears and a long bushy tail, it measures 474 feet from nose to tail. The precise age is difficult to determine, as it became overgrown almost to the point of invisibility and was extensively, though sensitively, re-dug in the nineteenth century. It has been speculated that it may be a fertility symbol although the theory that it once possessed an impressive *membrum virile* which was grassed over in more prudish times has been disproved.

Stiltius and Pibrovium

It was in the year 91 AD that a 28-year-old Roman centurion named Lucillus Stiltius sailed up the river to take command of the newly established Garrison of Pibrovium, set in a relatively flat and treeless area about 25 miles inland.

In his first report to the Emperor he noted that the natives were peaceable but seemed interested in little else but their pigs. He also thought that they were attempting to pay him homage for amongst their unsophisticated grunts the word "Stilt" could be clearly heard. However, other contemporary reports suggest that Stilt was already the local name for the river. Sadly, Lucillus never returned to Rome; on leaving at the end of his tour of duty he was drowned when his ship capsized off Gryatt Island.

Thus arose a controversy which has vexed scholars for generations. Did Stiltius give his name to the county or was it named after the river which has borne the name of Stilt since time immemorial?

Warlords and Wonder Woman

The Romans left Pibrovium some time in the late third or early fourth century and the area soon degenerated into a state of comparative anarchy (as indeed did most of England at that time). Eventually a few Saxons and Angles found their way there from the eastern regions and integrated with the local population, united it would seem by a common love of pigs.

During the sixth and seventh centuries, a number of Saxon warlords established small communities, raided one another's territories and generally made a nuisance of themselves but none came to prominence for long or gained anything like overall control of the area. Some of their names survive in ancient manuscripts: Aelred the Ancient (who died at the ripe old age of 68), Sodric the Straight, Snebric the Seasonal (not to be confused with Snebric the Sniveller), Wyddol the Witless, Winbald the Wary and Swilbert the Stinker, but little is recorded of their lives and exploits. It was not until the eighth century that these constantly warring factions began to coalesce into three distinct tribes.

Apster the Just, son of Agbert the Aimless, held sway in the upper reaches of the Stilt valley and the central plain south of the South Drones. In contrast to his father, he was known as a wise, thoughtful and purposeful man. His name first appears in the annals on the occasion of his marriage to Angstrid, daughter of Sodric, in 707.

Thyk the Imponderable, son of Baldric the Bedridden, held lands on the south coast, around present day Brobmore Regis, which had been in his family for generations. (The village of Thickness takes its name from him.) A tall man with a forked beard, he was in the habit of wearing a preposterous helmet surmounted by an enormous pair of bull's horns.

Bollin the Iniquitous, a man of uncertain parentage but frequently known as "the son of the Devil", had recently come to prominence in the west, on the borders of what is now Dongland. Among his more unpleasant habits was that of cutting out the tongues of those from whom he had stolen land. (The villages of Over, Nether and Silent Bolsacre owe their names to him.)

What none of these chieftains had managed to acquire was control of the Stilt estuary and the natural harbour of Stilhaven, which would obviously afford an enormous strategic advantage. By 730 all had established camps where their own territories bordered this coveted region - Apster on a hill overlooking the river (present day Apstrow), Thyk at what is now Cuggley and Bollin near Prokeworth - but, while numerous forays and minor skirmishes had taken place, no-one had conquered the region and the balance of power remained static.

Apster had for some time had spies in the guise of swineherds monitoring the activities of his rivals and began to formulate a plan. Clearly Bollin was a ruthless and amoral man who ruled by fear and terror. Thyk was vain, pompous and unpredictable. Neither could be trusted to form an alliance.

Thyk was known to frequent a tavern about three miles from his camp. One evening in May, a small band led by Apster's son Edric crept unnoticed into the tavern while Thyk made merry with his cronies, stole his helmet and made off with the group's horses in the direction of Thyk's camp. In the fading light, Edric sat on Thyk's horse wearing the helmet while his companions spread the word among Thyk's men that their leader had ordered them to march northwards at once and join Apster's army. By the time Thyk and his henchmen staggered back to the camp, it was almost deserted.

Meanwhile, Edric and his friends had ridden hard to the west, arriving at Bollin's camp an hour after nightfall. When all was quiet, they encircled the tents, lit a number of fires and made a hasty retreat, leaving the famous helmet lying on the ground. The result was predictable enough. Shortly after dawn, Bollin's men descended on Thyk's camp and slaughtered the few who remained there, including the chieftain himself.

By noon, news of the massacre had reached Apstrow and Apster had little difficulty in persuading Thyk's men to avenge their leader. Bollin's forces, still trying to mend their damaged tents, were hopelessly outnumbered and quickly dispatched. But one figure moved stealthily in the shadows, avoiding the main areas of fighting - Albric, son of Thyk crept from tent to tent until he met Bollin saddling his horse to flee. With a shout of triumph, he impaled the evil one with his sword, then hacked out his tongue with the warlord's own dagger. Sadly, as he stepped back to admire his handiwork, he was felled by a mighty axe blow.

Apster quickly assumed control. Thyk and Albric were given a hero's burial and the men who had taken part in the battle paid a handsome bonus to ensure their loyalty (conveniently financed by gold recovered from Bollin's headquarters). Bollin's tongue was nailed to a tree at Silent Bolsacre where it remained, routinely cursed and spat upon, until eaten by a rat some weeks later.

But the victory had cost Apster more than he bargained for. His son Edric had been severely wounded in the thigh and the right arm and was unable to ride, wield a sword or indulge other manly pursuits with the exception of falconry and downing prodigious quantities of ale and mead. Edric began to drink himself to oblivion and died barely two years later. By this time, Apster was approaching fifty years of age and a widower. He had no other son. But he did have a daughter....

Being an enlightened man, Apster had sent his daughter to be educated by progressive nuns on the continent. At 22, Ewburga was a feisty and self-assured young woman of strikingly good looks and possessing her father's good judgement and sense of justice - and she was a Christian.

Following her brother's death, she at once set about touring the countryside, winning the hearts and minds of the people, not just in the Stilt valley but across the central plain, the coastal areas where Thyk had ruled and into the hills of the north.

Within five years she had moved the administrative centre of her father's territories from present-day Apstrow to the abandoned garrison of Pibrovium, reasoning that if the Romans had considered it the ideal place from which to govern the surrounding lands they were probably not wrong. There was a chapel established some decades earlier by St Cedd during one of his missionary journeys. And she decreed that the city should be known by its alternative name of Stilchester.

Resolved to turn the temporary calm which Apster had brought to the area into a lasting peace, Ewburga strove to instil her Christian values into the populace who, being for the most part good natured, tolerant agriculture types more given to eating and drinking than making war, were happy to acquiesce. Over the next few years she brought in priests and monks to found what were to become the three great mediaeval religious institutions of Flover, Plean and Scrunton.

Rarely was Ewburga's authority challenged but on one occasion a group of elders at what would now be Sowport expressed some reluctance to pledge allegiance to a woman. "I am merely administering my father's territories" she replied. "Your father never conquered yon island" said one, gesticulating seawards. "Watch me" said Ewburga and, casting off her outer garments, she waded into the estuary and began swimming towards the island. A young man despatched to keep an eye on her was swept away by the current, but within the space of an hour and a quarter Ewburga had set foot on Gryatt Island. Gathering some timber, she erected a large makeshift cross on what is now the site of St Botolph's chapel. Then, pausing only to take bread and ale offered by the bemused inhabitants, she began to swim back to the mainland. At the entrance to the harbour she passed the young man lying safe but exhausted on the shore. By now a huge crowd had gathered with the elders on the bank. As she walked ashore they all fell to their knees, cheered heartily and hailed her as their queen.

Apster, in his declining years, was content to allow his daughter free reign. Indeed, it gave him much pride and satisfaction to see her consolidate by peaceable means what he had won by strength and guile. He died beside the river at Apstrow, gratefully commending his soul to his maker who had blessed him with a long and fruitful life and an extraordinarily capable heir.

Ewburga ruled for 45 years over an area which roughly corresponded to the old county of Stiltshire (i.e. minus Dongland) and they were years of peace and prosperity, funded by pig rearing, the wool trade in the north and shipping though the natural harbour of Stilhaven, all of which were to sustain the county for many centuries to come. Occasional skirmishes occurred with the wild folk who inhabited the rugged coastal areas to the south-west, but their disorganised forays rarely amounted to much.

On reaching three score years and ten, Ewburga handed control of the region to her cousin-once-removed Lunca (whose name is the origin of the popular surname Lunch and the town of Lonchelsea) and retired to Flover where she spent her remaining years in prayer and contemplation and died at the age of 84, apparently in the throes of a beatific vision.

Her religious institutions continued to flourish. From a tiny chapel and a farm, Scrunton Abbey grew until by the 11th century it was a magnificent edifice with accommodation for over 300 monks. Flover Priory comprised both a thriving nunnery and a seminary for training priests; indeed, it remains Stiltshire's theological college to this day. Plean Minster served as both a parish church for the surrounding area and home to a small community of friars.

By this time, much of the woodland of the central plain had been cleared and turned over to farming. It is known that pig-breeding was the chief occupation of the peasantry and at least two of the traditional Stiltshire breeds, the Prumeford Russet and the now rare Rimpleham, had their origins in late Saxon times. But the hills of the north remained bare and sparsely populated and it was there that one of Stiltshire's most enigmatic characters led his mostly solitary existence.

The Blessed Witta

The revered mystic Witta was born circa 930 AD, probably in what is now the village of Vazeworth. He entered holy orders as a young man, almost certainly at Scrunton Abbey, but left the cloisters around the age of forty and spent the rest of his life roaming the hills of north Stiltshire, observing the beauties of nature, pondering the mysteries of creation, healing the sick and dispensing succinct words of wisdom.

He died, aged about ninety, beside the natural well at what is now known as Witterspool. The local people could not bear to bury him, nor would any cleric say prayers for his soul, believing he was already granted a place at the right hand of God. It is said that his body did not decompose but slowly melted away into thin air.

Numerous miracles were attributed to him, both during his lifetime and posthumously; indeed, the aforesaid well is even now believed to have curative properties. [See also the stories behind the Hump and the Bowl of Gruel inn signs later in this book.]

Many of his sayings survive, having been handed down orally for several generations and then recorded by the monks of Scrunton in a beautiful illuminated manuscript, *Dictis Insignia Beatus Wittus*, which fortunately survived the Dissolution and is today the most priceless document in the extensive library of St Cedd's College.

Fruits of Wisdom

As the sweetest fruit groweth beneath the coarsest scrub, so cometh the sweetest wisdom under adversity.

The tiny, juicy fruits known to the local people as wittaberries (otherwise called whinberries, bilberries or wild blueberries) which grow in profusion on the North and South Drones would have formed a staple part of the holy man's diet during the summer but, as anyone who has tried picking them will know, the coarse ground-hugging bushes do not yield their fruit easily.

The Hedgehog

Blessed is the hedgehog, for he hath the bread of Heaven before his snout and the armour of God upon his back.

Elderflowers

The Spirit of God bloometh in the hearts of the simple, pale and fragrant as the elderflower, and His wine is of great strength.

The Caterpillar

Despise not the caterpillar, for it shall become a thing of great beauty.
Look not scornfully upon the body, for thou knowest not the soul within.

The Badger

Pursue the way of righteousness, as the noble badger followeth his well-trodden path and will not turn aside nor suffer any hindrance to be put in his way.

These are just some of many sayings which illustrate Witta's ability to see the divine in the simple things of life and to draw potent analogies from nature.

The Gift of Water

Water is the eternal gift of God,
For it gathereth in the clouds of Heaven,
It falleth as the gentle rain upon the hills,
It settleth as dew upon the heather
And it riseth in the clear, cold spring.
I drink of the well and am refreshed,
Then I pass it to the earth again.

The chattering rill runneth to the river

And the river to the great sea.
Thus it is with the Spirit,
For it moveth freely upon the earth
And refresheth the soul.
All we are as drops flung from the mighty ocean,
And thence in the love of God we shall return.

Witta's reflections on the cycle of life, death, rebirth and eternity.

The Brotherhood of Man

Every man is an island
But we are all in the same sea.

Did Witta perhaps anticipate John Donne by six centuries?

On Enlightenment

Put the ocean into a bottle,
Bind the hills with a lock of hair,
Then gather eggs and make an hearty breakfast.

This was the swift answer given to a young monk who asked the aged Witta how to attain enlightenment. There is something of the koan about it. Indeed, it has often been noted that Witta had much in common with the great Zen masters who were his contemporaries, although it is most unlikely that he could have had any contact with them or their teachings.

Witta's Benediction

God bless thee and grant thee
The eyes of an hawk,
The ears of a dog,
The feet of an horse,
The belly of an hog,
And the mind of a stone.

The Rev'd Sidney Otter, in his commentary on the works of Witta (Collected Sermons No. 23), remarked: "This simple benison at first caused me great perplexity. Whereas the gifts craved in the first three clauses are clear enough, what are we to make of the last two? The belly of an hog methinks is not to imply greed but rather the capacity of the omnivorous pig to enjoy whatever the Lord in His bounty sets before him. As for the mind of a stone, it is clear, long-sighted and unchanging. Stones are great reservoirs of spiritual energy. They do not burden themselves with the trifling concerns and ambitions of men. They take no thought for the morrow, nor the day after, for their ways are eternal."

Odfranc, first Bishop of Stilchester

Odfranc was a Norman cleric, a distant relative of William the Conqueror. His early life was marked by a precocious childhood, a distinguished academic career and an unsavoury incident in which he single-handedly quelled a peasant rebellion by mashing the heads of the ring-leaders with his clerical mace.

A few years after the Norman conquest he set sail for England in the hope of acquiring a generous benefice from Uncle Willie. He was allocated the newly created see of Stilchester.

Arriving in the city with his entourage of cooks, clerks and soldiers, he found a small stone chapel on the western bank of the River Stilt administered by a Saxon cleric by the name of Wogarde. Having first attended to the essential task of creating suitably lavish accommodation for himself in the form of a small palace across the river, he then set about his role of overseeing the area's spiritual well-being with enthusiasm. His first task was to banish Wogarde from the city; his second to have the Saxon chapel demolished, and the third to impose a 50% tax on the inhabitants of the city and surrounding countryside for the purpose of building a magnificent edifice to the glory of God and the Norman Empire.

Thus it was that in the year 1084 a team of skilled Norman masons, carpenters and other craftsmen arrived in Stilchester to begin construction of the new chapel at Odfranc's chosen site on the east bank of the Stilt. This was to be the first stage in the building of a mighty cathedral. In order to demonstrate that he meant business, the Bishop decreed that his men would begin work on Monday morning and that he would celebrate Mass in the new building on the following Sunday.

By Monday evening the foundations had been laid. On Tuesday the walls began to rise rapidly as the stones from the former Saxon chapel were heaved into place. By Thursday afternoon the carpenters, having cut all the beams for the roof, were beginning to haul them aloft and set them in their niches on the now complete walls. Odfranc, watching progress from his palace, afforded himself a smug smile as the work progressed. In the taverns, where the ale had been reduced to half price (except to Normans) to allow the poor over-taxed citizens to afford it, people muttered darkly.

On Friday morning Wogarde, who had been brought news of these goings-on and had left his retreat in the hills to the north-east, strode grimly through the city gate and marched straight to the Bishop's palace with, so 'twas said, a grey shrouded figure following silently in his wake. The furious cleric burst into the chamber where the Bishop sat at meat, thumped the table and denounced Odfranc for blasphemy on the grounds that by presuming to finish his work of creation in six days he was setting himself on a par with the Lord.

Before the startled Bishop could call the guards, Wogarde was gone and minutes later was seen to leave the city and return whence he came with the same mysterious figure at his shoulder. One or two old folk who as young children had seen the Blessed Witta shortly before he died were prepared to swear upon oath that Wogarde's mysterious companion was none other than the venerable hermit himself.

When Odfranc, having spent a troubled night, went to inspect the work on Saturday morning, all was not well. The carpenters were having trouble with several of the main timbers for the roof, which failed to meet in the middle. They had already made one set of replacements for the offending beams and these had proved no better fit than the originals. Having checked and re-checked their measurements, they set about hewing a third set from their now dwindling stock of timber.

After a lighter lunch than usual, the Bishop returned to find that the new timbers still lacked half an inch at the crucial point. Alternating between frenzied rage and abject despair, he first threatened them with amputation of their right arms if they failed to complete the task, and minutes later offered them a substantial bonus in gold if they succeeded. Thus inspired, the carpenters set about making another set of beams while the slaters stood by to cover the timbers in record time the moment they became stable and the makers of ecclesiastical furniture began bringing the holy table and other artefacts into the building despite the risk of their handiwork, or indeed their persons, being damaged by careless movement above.

As afternoon turned to evening, Odfranc, having not dared to watch the proceedings for the last few hours, returned in trepidation to the site. The roof was still non-existent; the eighth set of timbers, roughly hewn from a scrawny and hastily felled ash, the supply of seasoned oak having run out at the sixth set, stood atop the walls like the ribs of a recumbent skeleton with a gap of several inches where the sternum ought to be. All around, carpenters were collapsing from exhaustion, many having additionally been severely beaten by irate slaters who saw their bonus evaporating due to the apparent incompetence of their woodworking colleagues. The masons who were to have placed the cross and finials on the roof had long since given up and taken themselves off to the alehouse. As the daylight faded, the awful truth dawned upon Odfranc that his mighty plan had been thwarted. He stood alone on the river bank, gazing disconsolately westward as the last red glimmer of the sun slipped below the horizon.

In the morning, he was wakened by a distant sound as of joyful singing. Stumbling to the window, he looked out towards that wretched building whose opulent but starkly unfinished shape had haunted him all night long. It was not there. Rubbing his eyes, he opened the window to take in the wider vista. Sure enough, the site was bare of chapel, building materials, or anything apart from a patch of mud.

Slowly he swivelled his gaze to the other side of the river, whence came the noise of singing and rejoicing. There stood the old Saxon chapel in all its glory exactly where it had stood before and surrounded by many hundreds of townsfolk, the assembled congregation being several times the capacity of the little church. And there was Father Wogarde, resplendent in gold robes, preparing to celebrate the Eucharist.

How the chapel had crossed the river and reconstructed itself in the space of a single night has never been explained. Some claimed to have seen things on the Saturday evening: boatmen bringing rafts quietly up the river, dozens of the best Saxon craftsmen from the villages for miles around assembling in the taverns. Others maintained the task was not humanly possible and hinted at a more numinous explanation.

Only one thing is certain: from that day forward Bishop Odfranc was a changed man. That evening he put on sackcloth and went to the chapel to make his confession to Wogarde and seek absolution for his sins of pride and avarice. This Wogarde graciously did and blessed his persecutor. The chapel was gloomy and witnesses few but more than one attested that not two, but four hands were laid upon the bishop.

From then on, the two men worked in co-operation, and shortly afterwards began to make plans for the building of a new cathedral, not for the purpose of mere ostentation, but because it became impracticable to conduct services for a combined Saxon and Norman congregation which could only be accommodated in the open air or in five or six sittings in the little chapel. Furthermore, there was no dispute over the fact that the mother church of Stiltshire should remain on the west bank of the Stilt where higher authority than Odfranc decreed it should be and where it remains to this day.

Odfranc lived a further 24 years and committed many acts of great piety. He dwelt in a modest room close to the cathedral so as to be always on hand to minister to the spiritual or temporal needs of his flock. But just occasionally he could be seen in the evening standing on the river bank gazing ruefully into the sunset.

For many centuries the Bishop and Sunset Inn has stood on the north side of the cathedral close as a constant reminder of these strange events.

[Odfranc's family crest was a red monkey – hence the mitred red monkey who sits atop the arms of Stiltshire.]

The Diocese of Stilchester

The episcopal see of Stilchester has changed little since the eleventh century. On the death of Odfranc, Wogarde succeeded him as Bishop of Stilchester. The current incumbent, the Right Rev'd Spencer Kettle, is the 67th to hold the title.

The modern Diocese roughly follows the boundaries of the county of Stiltshire - or rather, the county boundary has evolved to follow the ecclesiastical one (including the former county of Dongland which was always part of the Diocese), except for the parish of Henbrowe, whose Rector and congregation were excommunicated by the eighth Bishop, Maximus, in 1169.

The cause of this unprecedented event was an enormous flock of geese which roamed freely over the churchyard and the village green. Whenever the right reverend gentleman or one of his Archdeacons visited the church, they were driven away by the frenzied honking and wing flapping of several hundred of the creatures. Bishop Maximus, annoyed at this affront to his dignity, requested the Rector to remove the birds from consecrated ground. When the latter refused, on the grounds that the geese were a security device and kept the grass short, the Bishop denounced the Rector as being in league with the devil, the geese being his familiars, and promptly declared the parish out of communion with the see of Stilchester. After some years in the spiritual wilderness, Henbrowe was rescued by the bishop of the neighbouring diocese, who undertook to oversee the cure of souls in exchange for a regular supply of plump geese for his table.

Had these events occurred in Flunt, or Cuggley, or almost anywhere else, this situation might well have pertained for some centuries, but would no doubt have long since been amended by some reorganisation or "rationalisation", for the bureaucratic mind abhors an enclave. But since Henbrowe lies conveniently on the northern edge of the county, the anomaly has been allowed to stand for over 800 years.

The Diocese is divided into seven Archdeaconries: Cauldby, Scrunton, Plean, Apstrow, Flover, Brinceton and Spruntley, plus the city of Stilchester which comes under the direct jurisdiction of the Bishop. There are two Suffragan bishoprics, Eyvesborough and Brinceton.

In the middle ages, a fine musical tradition developed around the three great religious institutions of Stilchester Cathedral, Scrunton Abbey and Flover Priory, each of which had its own distinctive style of plain chant known respectively as the Stilchester, Scrunton and Flover modes. Scrunton Abbey, alas, has been a ruin since the dissolution of the monasteries but Flover Priory escaped destruction by a curious quirk of fate (see the Oxbake-Jupton feud) and is now a theological college.

The Reformation caused little trouble in Stiltshire. Clergy were broadly sympathetic to the views of the continental reformers and such dubious practices as the selling of indulgences had been viewed with suspicion for decades. Bishop Brazier was for the most part happy to implement Cranmer's liturgical changes and to endorse his views on the True Presence. However he balked at the suggestion of predestination implicit in the Archbishop's doctrine of salvation: "If my Lord of Canterbury do think, as it seemeth, that our salvation or damnation be pre-ordained, then I am out of step with him, for I cannot but believe that the Lord God hath given us minds that we may come to him, or nay, of our own volition."

During the brief reign of Mary, lip service was paid to the Catholic revival, which was not difficult; the vestments had only been discreetly hidden away and Latin motets had been sung throughout Edward's reign, there being no reason to sacrifice art on the altar of liturgical correctness.

Today most parishes may be described as broad church, albeit leaning towards the liberal catholic rather than the evangelical.

The Cathedral

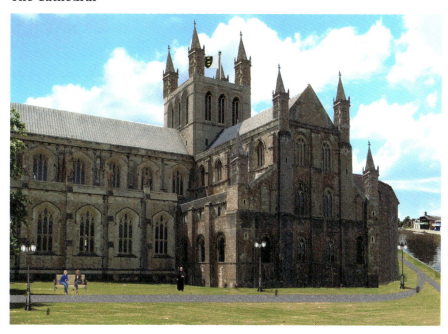

The Cathedral Church of St Cedd and the Holy Rood, begun in 1084 by Odfranc and Wogarde, is a massive edifice of typical Norman design with a long nave and a squat central tower and a chancel added later in the perpendicular style. Since that extension and the extensive remodelling of the interior completed under Bishop Grantham in 1440, it has changed little.

There are chapels dedicated to St Anthony, patron saint of swineherds and St

Ewburga, daughter of Apster the Just who instigated the conversion of her father's pagan subjects to Christianity. Chantry chapels contain the mortal remains of Bishops Odfranc, Wogarde, Avunculus and Grantham, as well as those of Erasmus Sprunt, founder of St Cedd's College and Roger de Pailey, first Duke of Stiltshire. The choir features some exquisite woodwork, including stalls, misericords and the great rood screen, all carved in Jupton oak.

The organ is a magnificent four manual instrument, the *magnum opus* of the Eyvesborough organ builder Thomas Carnforth the younger (1721-1800). In the tower hangs a noble ring of 12 bells in the key of B flat from the Prokeworth foundry of Craddock and Oates (1752); the 44 cwt Tenor bell bears the name *Grantham*. There is also an unusual clock, powered by rainwater which collects in a tank on the top of the tower and filters down through an ingenious regulating mechanism. In times of drought it has been customary to send choristers with buckets up the 169 steps to replenish the tank.

Among the cathedral's long line of distinguished Masters of Music are the eclectic renaissance composer, Thomas Peltigrewe (c1540-1619), who produced a large output of motets for both the English and Latin rites, and Dr Bertram Lunch (1834-1903); "Lunch in D" is still performed at Evensong every Thursday. Today the baton is carried by Dr Ashley Pencil. Over the centuries, the highest standards of choral singing have been maintained by some notable singers, particularly in the bass section, including Reuben Credence, the legendary Harry Bromley with his famous bottom B flat (as mentioned in the song "Oxbake Ale") and in the present day Quainton Rhodes.

Churches

The Diocese boasts many fine churches including:
St Mary the Virgin, Eyvesborough, with its splendid flying buttresses, built on the proceeds of the woollen trade;
St Benedict, Apstrow whose tall and imposing tower, set at an angle to the nave, looks squarely down the mile-long Avenue towards the smaller church of St Mary Magdalene by the river;
St Gabriel, Apstrow Angelica with its 49 stone angels decorating the tower and the nave;
St Andrew, Stilhaven, whose stout weather-beaten tower stands on the edge of the quay;
St Barnabas, Clabworth, famed for the intricate carving of its pews and roof beams;
St Cecelia, Lydegar Decorum with its ornate dome and curious arrangement of three spires;
St Mildred, Prumeford, with its mediaeval fresco "The Adoration of the Porci";
and the tiny chapel of St Botolph on Gryatt Island, its tower partly hewn out of the rock.

The City of Stilchester

The county town of Stiltshire bestrides the River Stilt at the site of the Roman garrison of Pibrovium. In Saxon times it supported a thriving community of artisans and provided a marketplace for the farmers and woodsmen of the surrounding countryside. Its importance grew with the creation of the see of Stilchester in 1084 and the establishment of the University in 1311.

Nowadays, Stilchester retains the air of an archetypal English cathedral city and seat of learning. There is little industrialisation and many mediaeval buildings remain along with fragments of the Roman walls. Narrow, winding strips of wooded parkland meander along the river banks, past the colleges, churches and inns. The Cathedral stands on the west bank of the Stilt, overlooking extensive water meadows. There are several fine churches, including St Anthony's with its octagonal tower and pig gargoyles, St Candida's where the thrushes sing in the churchyard, St Radegund's with its labyrinthine and seriously creepy crypt, the little round church of St Orry and the ancient chapel of All Souls-without-Sowgate.

The magnificent Sievewrights' Hall was built for the Worshipful Company of Sievewrights in the 1820s when the sieve and colander industry was at its height, replacing an earlier timber building; nowadays it mainly serves as a venue for banquets, concerts and beer festivals.

A long, crooked row of half-timbered cottages, the Quiritic Almshouses have provided relief to the poor and suffering of the city since 1477 and today serve as a rest home for retired priests and lay clerks.

The Hymnodical Library houses an unparalleled collection of liturgical music and the Ezra Rhodes Museum of Stiltshire Lore offers a fascinating insight into the history and folklore of the county, based on the researches of Rev'd Ezra Rhodes (1867-1949), while the Museum of Porcine Husbandry celebrates its long tradition of pig keeping.

Completed in 2000, the octagonal Opera House is, despite its name, a venue for various genres of music and home to the Stilchester Philharmonic Orchestra. The Columbine Theatre has an interesting history, having been twice burnt down - accidentally in 1775 by a raucous party of sailors smoking and drinking in the 'gods' when they found the play too boring and deliberately in 1925 by an evangelical minister protesting at the "inherent immorality of thespians".

For relaxation one can walk in the Water Meadows or Erasmus Park or take the waters at the splendid Victorian Municipal Baths. For refreshment there are 45 pubs, from the ancient Bishop and Sunset, the Rabbit Pie, the Gill Pot and the Bell and Bladder to a newly-opened micro-pub, the Loud Bassoon.

Transportation is provided by a comprehensive network of tramways, although the visitor will note that the north-west quarter is devoid of tramlines. This is because when the system was first proposed in 1918 the Dean and Chapter refused to countenance the prospect of noisy trams running close to the Cathedral precincts. (Today's trams, while retaining their traditional appearance and distinctive dark green and cream livery, are comparatively quiet.) There are no internal bus routes in the city, although buses run from the tram depot to nearby towns and villages.

Trains run from Stilchester Central to Stiltford, Gruntlington, Apstrow, Stilhaven, Brobmore Regis and Japhetstow. The Stilchester to Eyvesborough line fell foul of that pusillanimous bean counter Dr Beeching but has been gradually brought back into use by the Mid-Stilts Railway Company; only the section from Aggerby Junction to Kings Pebberworth remains unrestored. Stilchester West station still stands empty, a sad reminder of the abortive Stilchester, Oxbake and Spruntley Railway project begun by Giovanni Giacometti, an Italian engineer who married a local girl and settled in Oxbake.

Following the reopening of the Prokeworth and Chineham Canal, a new marina was built where the canal joins the river on the southern edge of the city. This, with its own pub the Gullet, provides a convenient starting point for boaters embarking on the "Stiltshire Ring".

The University of Stilchester comprises three* colleges:

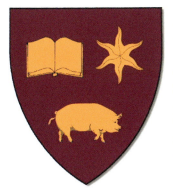

St Cedd's - founded in 1311 by Erasmus Sprunt, who also gave his name to the town of Spruntley (or possibly vice-versa) and named after the saint who first established a chapel in the city. It is located on the west bank of the Stilt a few hundred yards south of the Cathedral. The original buildings are arranged around a quadrangle, apart from the chapel with its imposing tower containing a fine ring of ten bells.

Old College - founded in 1313 by Bishop Avunculus. It is said that when Sprunt announced his plans to endow the city with a seat of learning, the Bishop was rather peeved at not having thought of the idea himself, so he quickly followed suit and named his foundation "Old" in the hope that people would assume it predated St Cedd's. It stands on the east bank near Bishops Bridge. In 1742 the tower of the chapel fell down and remained a pile of rubble, beloved of generations of students. Plans to reinstate it for the millennium met with bitter controversy until a compromise was reached – the tower was rebuilt with new stone on the opposite side of the chapel while the old stones were left exactly where they had lain for 260 years.

Stangley Hall - founded in 1537 by Sir Edmund Stangley to support the flowering of the arts and sciences in the Renaissance. It is built in Elizabethan style and stands on the east bank near Erasmus Park.

In 1606, the three colleges were formally incorporated by royal charter into the University of Stilchester and continued to maintain standards of educational excellence that were the envy of the world for the next two and a half centuries.

The late nineteenth century was perhaps the darkest chapter in the University's history, with many academics drinking to excess and consumption of the esoteric monastic beverage Aqua Discorpus reaching record levels. Then, over a period of eighteen months in 1888-9, six dons were murdered, each found dissolving in acid in his own bathtub. No motive was apparent, the dead men having no obvious connection, and the culprit was never apprehended.

Today, all three colleges enjoy an enviable reputation. St Cedd's is perhaps most highly regarded for history, philosophy, divinity and the classics, Old College for medicine, mathematics and law, while Stangley Hall specialises in music and the sciences. Loyalty to the institution is intense with the vast majority of dons being alumni of one or other of the colleges.

Relations between "town and gown" are cordial and there is much friendly rivalry between students and apprentices. The annual Boat Race is held on the first Saturday after Trinity, when teams from the three colleges compete against the Sievewrights, the Swineherds and the Brewers.

Another highlight of the academic calendar is the Michaelmas Ale and Fig Contest. In this ancient ritual, dating from the 14th century, each contestant has to alternately drink a guzzock (a mediaeval drinking vessel made from a cured pig's bladder and holding two and a ninth pints) of strong ale or porter and eat seven ripe figs without a pause until he is unable to take any more. The record, set by Henry Beef of Old College in 1797, stands at 12 guzzocks of ale and 81 figs. Filling the bladders with ale as fast as the contestants can empty them is a highly-skilled task, traditionally practised by medical students, while the quantities are verified by umpires from the Town Clerk's office.

The 17th century Observatory, near the Cathedral, is owned by the University. Although not ideally placed or equipped for modern astronomical research, it still offers spectacular views to amateur stargazers during the early hours when the streetlights are dimmed.

* Or was it four? Undergraduates, particularly of St Cedd's, may speak of another academic establishment known as Scroterhouse. Although "going to Scroterhouse" is normally regarded as a figure of speech - and not generally complimentary - there are written references to it in the annals of St Cedd's and the idea that a fourth college once existed has been taken seriously, particularly in the early twentieth century when certain academics even quoted the dates of its foundation (1398) and dissolution (1523). However, subsequent researches and archaeological excavations in the city have failed to find any conclusive evidence of the buildings.

By and large, Stiltshire people are among the most amenable and amiable folk one could hope to meet. All the more strange then that the villagers of Oxbake and Jupton regard one another with a mutual hatred of such vehemence. They will not speak to anyone from the other village unless it be to curse them, nor will they set foot in each other's territory unless to commit acts of terrorism and sabotage.

To uncover the roots of this extraordinary animosity, we must go back to the year 1435. The great Cathedral of Stilchester, begun by Bishop Odfranc, was then nearing completion in the form in which we know it today and required many tons of seasoned oak for supporting the roof and furnishing the interior. The obvious source of timber would have been Oxbake Woods, a patch of ancient broad-leaved forest with a plentiful supply of mature trees and barely five miles distant. However, the elders of Oxbake reckoned without the persuasiveness of a certain Guy de Wiberton, parish clerk of Jupton.

First he attempted to influence Bishop Grantham and other notables by publishing a treatise entitled *Pro Quercus Juptonensis* extolling the supposedly superior qualities of Jupton oak. Finally he bribed the Dean and Chapter with 15 saddles of venison, 4 swans, 65 brace of woodcock and an hogshead of ale, not to mention sundry crayfish, bottles of mead and other delicacies. History does not record whether these items constituted one enormous banquet or were distributed as gifts for domestic consumption. Suffice it to say that his tactics were successful and the contract was awarded to Jupton.

The following year, Jupton's little church of St Ethelburga was mysteriously destroyed by fire. Although arson by the disgruntled people of Oxbake was strongly suspected, nothing was proven. To make matters worse, when it came to the re-building, all mature oaks in the Jupton area had already gone to Stilchester and they were forced to buy from Oxbake at whatever price the latter would agree to which, needless to say, was not cheap. Matters came to a head when a dozen Jupton woodmen took it into their heads to go and cut their own timber from Oxbake Woods. They were discovered by a band of their local counterparts and a bloody axe battle ensued which left seven men dead and many more limbless or badly mutilated.

A century or so later, during the dissolution of the monasteries, a platoon of demolition men arrived at Scrunton Abbey and within a few days had reduced that magnificent edifice to the empty shell which it remains today. Having completed their unholy task, they set out for their next destination, Flover Priory, and being uncertain of its whereabouts happened to ask a passing Jupton man for directions. He, divining their intentions and being a quick-witted fellow, gave them very detailed directions - to Oxbake.

A day later they arrived at St Benedict's Church and, despite its being not quite what they had anticipated, set about their work. They were interrupted by the Rector who eventually managed to convince them that they had come to the wrong place. He promised to direct them to Flover, bid them stay overnight in the inn at the parish's expense and in the morning sent them on their way - to Jupton. On arrival at St Ethelburga's they encountered the Sexton, whom they immediately recognised as the man who had led them astray earlier, and beat him to within an inch of his life. Being in no mood for further games and tiring of being sent back and forth across the county, they set fire to the rood screen, smashed font, altar and statuary and, taking a few relics as evidence, returned to report their business in Stiltshire complete. Thus was Flover Priory saved for posterity.

Far from improving with the passage of time, relations between the two villages became ever more violent. Over the years there have been countless beatings and abductions, occasional murders and numerous arson attacks including the destruction of both churches three times and of the newly built Oxbake station in 1888, which act effectively put an end to Giovanni Giacometti's planned Stilchester, Oxbake and Spruntley railway. Natural disasters such as the failure of the Jupton harvest in 1837 have been claimed as divine intervention on behalf of the other side.

Today, any Jupton man will swear that he would rather die of thirst than permit a drop of Oxbake ale to pass his lips, which is music to the ears of Swallows of Eyvesborough who have maintained a total monopoly in the area since Jupton's own brewery closed in the 1930s.

Children learn their tribal identity at their mother's bosom and are chanting nasty nursery rhymes about the enemy almost as soon as they can talk. Burly P.E. teachers have been known to quake in their plimsolls at the mere prospect of refereeing the annual football match between Oxbake Grammar and Jupton High, a spectacle of blood-letting and savagery exceeded in ferocity only by the girls' hockey fixture.

[One of the most bizarre consequences of the feud is the Oxbake Canal. When work began on the Jupton Canal (actually an arm of the Mid-Stilts Canal) in 1791, Oxbake naturally had to have one too. The six and a half mile waterway runs from the River Stilt just north of Stilchester via two locks to the village centre then continues for a further 2.7 miles before it stops abruptly. An ambitious plan to extend it to Spruntley was abandoned soon after construction started but work could not stop until the canal was a full furlong longer than the Jupton Canal.]

The title of Duke of Stiltshire was first bestowed upon Sir Roger de Pailey (1310-65) in 1341 in recognition of his distinguished service during Edward III's French campaign of 1339-40. With funds largely acquired from his work in France, the first Duke set about enlarging the family home into a magnificent edifice known as Clamburton Castle.

His descendants for the next two centuries proved to be a succession of worthy if undistinguished noblemen with the exception of the Fifth Duke, Henshawe de Pailey (1413-36), who inherited the title, entered into the holy estate of matrimony and died in a jousting tournament all within the space of five days, although not without managing to sire a son and heir in the meantime. His cousin, Allard de Pailey, was urged to seize the title but nobly insisted on waiting a few months to see whether a true heir was forthcoming.

The Sixth Duke, Arthur (1437-79), having thus succeeded to the title at birth, grew up to be not only a wise landowner but also a shrewd merchant who did much to enhance the fortunes of the wool-rearing areas in the north-east and the burgeoning town of Eyvesborough, in recognition of which his eldest son was granted the filial title of Marquess of Eyvesborough.

Unfortunately, the Ninth Duke, Balham de Pailey (1507-1588), proved to be the last. Scarcely had he turned forty when, following the death of his second wife in childbirth, he allowed his hair and beard to grow to unseemly proportions and began to behave somewhat oddly. He was wont to disappear into Bayconhurst Woods or Knorrley Forest for days, even weeks on end, during which times, if seen at all, he was observed by local peasants running naked among the trees, feeding upon berries or enjoying the company of wild animals.

On Easter Sunday 1558, he stood before the Bishop in Stilchester Cathedral and pronounced that "God is an ass". A man of less exalted status might have been arrested forthwith for blasphemy. As it was, the Duke merely walked out of the Cathedral, leaving the congregation aghast, and rode home to Clamburton. Shortly afterwards, exercising his prerogative as patron of the parish, he dismissed the Rector and declared the church out-of-bounds to the villagers.

The following year, the Bishop, being somewhat perturbed at this turn of events and having heard nothing further from the wayward Duke, sent a canon to investigate. The cleric returned with an alarming report: "These past seventeen months, so I am told, his Grace hath suffered to be kept in the sanctuary an he-ass of monstrous proportions. This I have seen with mine own eyes and have smelled the stench which is loathsome. Lately he hath built an altar of the beast's dung, upon which he doth set a fair linen cloth and thereupon doth administer a travesty of the Blessed Sacrament unto himself and such of his retinue as can stomach his vile ways, notwithstanding that the ass himself doth regularly kick over this shrine of profanity as though the poor creature were the only representative of the Almighty in that dreadful place."

This news proved too much for the Bishop, who immediately sought a warrant from the Queen to have the Duke arrested and tried on a charge of heresy. The trial began on 16th November 1559 in the Sievewrights' Hall. Under examination, the Duke insisted that his bizarre beliefs were the highest truth known to man and had been vouchsafed to him over the course of two decades by an extra-terrestrial being known as Morfark. After seven days, a unanimous verdict of guilty was obtained and the Duke sentenced to death, which punishment was later commuted to life imprisonment on account of his undeniable insanity.

At the Sovereign's command, the wretched heretic was stripped of his title which then fell into abeyance, although his eldest son, Alford de Pailey, who had for some years distanced himself from his father's activities, was allowed to retain the Marquessate of Eyvesborough in perpetuity. Clamburton Castle was razed to the ground and the church of Holy Trinity set ablaze as an act of purification and rebuilt at the expense of the Marquess, who then retired to his own home at Lower Crenton Place where the de Paileys have resided ever since.

Balham de Pailey lived another thirty years as a prisoner on Gryatt Island, where he thrived on the company of rats and spiders and claimed to be in regular communion with his celestial mentor, Morfark.

Thus came the Duchy of Stilchester to its ignominious end. The title has never been revived but through the ensuing centuries the Marquesses of Eyvesborough and the name of de Pailey have been bywords for gentlemanly conduct, philanthropy and military valour with never a hint of scandal - apart from the time when Lady Genevieve eloped with Saucy Sam the pirate.

The current Marquess, Bedford de Pailey, is the 19th to hold the title.

[See the de Pailey family tree at the end of the book.]

Thomas Fetlock

Thomas Fetlock was born in Smoatham around 1498, the third son of a master swineherd. It seems likely that he was a chorister at Stilchester Cathedral and probably studied the organ there under William Mayce around 1511-15.

At the age of 23, he was engaged as Master of Musicke to the Eighth Duke of Stiltshire at Clamburton Castle and remained in the employment of the de Pailey family for most of his working life. He appears to have been well liked by the old Duke, from whom he received the generous gift of a substantial house on the Clamburton estate on the occasion of his marriage in 1529 to Elizabeth Femur, daughter of the Rector of Clabworth, and there is no doubt that he was on extremely good terms with the eccentric Balham de Pailey who succeeded to the dukedom in 1536.

During his career, Fetlock composed a considerable amount of instrumental music for performance at Clamburton, most of which has not survived. He is better known for his madrigals, which he apparently wrote for his own amusement, setting texts of his own devising. A typical example is "Sweet Philomela":

Sweet Philomela, for her my heart sighs,
Of all comely maidens she beareth the prize,
Fairest of face and yet fairer of thighs.
Fa la la la la la la la, fa la la la la la la la,
Fa la la la la la la la, fa la la la.

Fair Helen's face launched a thousand great ships,
Yet Philomel's charms those of Helen eclipse,
Ruddy her cheeks and so sturdy her hips.
Fa la la la la la la la, fa la la la la la la la,
Fa la la la la la la la, fa la la la.

Similar sentiments are expressed in "Young men who a-courting go, if ye be but wise, look not on a maiden's face but only on her thighs." Other titles among his better-known madrigals are "When Cupid sleeping Venus spies" and "When Phyllis runs Amyntas cries". Indeed, all his secular choral works may be said to follow a predictable theme - with the singular exception of a rather strange glee for male voices: "Why is my beard prone to bifurcation?".

Fetlock wrote little religious music and was probably not encouraged to do so by his employer. His few motets are mostly settings of texts which are, to say the least, unconventional and generally owe more to Fetlock's imagination than any accurate rendering of the scriptures or theological exposition: "Behold, the Queen of Sheba lies", "When David on Bathsheba bathing cast his eyes", "The Baptist's head became Salome's prize".

His career more or less came to an end when the Ninth Duke was found guilty of heresy and banished to Gryatt Island. Fetlock's sorrow at the disgrace of his master is summed up in the doleful march, "The Duke of Stiltshire's Exile", which he composed at the time. By all accounts he did not get on with the Duke's son, Alford de Pailey, and left the Clamburton estate to live in a modest cottage in his native Smoatham, where he bred pigs and died in relative obscurity in 1586.

The Duke of Stiltshire's Exile — Thomas Fetlock

The conductor and musicologist Timothy Berdick-George has written (extracts from the sleeve notes to the album "Fetlock and Fancy Free"):

Whilst Fetlock's dates and oeuvre place him firmly in the English Madrigal School, albeit at a rickety desk in one of the lower forms, his eclectic style is inextricably rooted in his Stiltshire upbringing and agricultural ancestry.

There is always in his music a modal, folky undercurrent which evokes the gentle rolling hills and porcine pastures of his homeland. His lyrical melodies float over a homespun ground-bass like the cock crowing upon a dunghill, while his uncompromising false relations impinge upon the ear, as redolent of the harsh realities of peasant life as the eructations of a flatulent pig.

His counterpoint sparkles with all the life and laughter of village boys and girls, sunshine, cider and haystacks. His simple verses, penned by his own hand, reveal a charming rustic sensuality combined with a recourse to recurring themes in which a psychologist might find ample evidence of a pathologically obsessive nature.

And yet... there is a profoundly spiritual side to Fetlock's work which struggles to make sense of his entire ethos; the simple orison of a man who knows his bones are but dust and his entrails worm fodder yet feels unerringly within his solar plexus the faint flame of eternity.

On a hill top, high above Hazedale in the North Drones where sheep graze unhindered and the little river Haze runs its chattering course down towards Hazzock, a tall, sturdy tower stands silhouetted against the baleful skies. This lonely edifice is no mere folly; it commemorates one of the most singular events in military history, a conflict remarkable for the fact that not a single man was killed or even seriously injured.

It took place during the Civil War. Now, Stiltshire, as you might suppose, was staunchly royalist; not so much because the people were loyal to the King, although of course they were, but because, since time immemorial, Stiltshire folk have strenuously opposed puritanism, communism, capitalism in its more extreme manifestations, bureaucracy or any other ideology which threatened to curtail their enjoyment of the important things in life. That being the case, most of the county remained undisturbed during those troubled times while Cauldby, that grey granite fortress of a town in the north-east, stood guard as it always had done against the incursions of parliamentarians from the north. There the Royal Stiltshire Regiment fought a number of noble campaigns, culminating in the bloody battle of Cauldby Moor when many men were slain.

In the aftermath of that terrible conflict, the roundhead army withdrew over the border and regrouped. Within days their commander, Colonel Boff, decided to make a detour eastward, march down the Eyve valley and attempt to take Eyvesborough by surprise. Fortunately, the first stirrings of the camp at dawn were observed by the ever-watchful dale shepherds, who reported back to General Sir Charles Wyrecroft at Cauldby. He immediately mobilised his troops and sent word to the Marquess of Eyvesborough whose private army was stationed in Great Ryming. Their combined forces assembled in Hazedale that evening and, at first light, swarmed over the hill and descended upon the parliamentarian host as it passed through Goadinger.

The village of Goadinger consists of many steep, narrow streets set on a rugged and heavily wooded hillside. Under such conditions, it was inevitable that the fighting took place in small pockets spread over a wide area. Such was the profusion of potential hiding places that anyone seeing a flashing blade or a pointing gun barrel could easily crawl under a bush, duck into a doorway or sprint down some alley or other. What might have been the only fatal blow of the day was deflected when the tip of the assailant's sword caught on the low stone lintel of the lych-gate, allowing the intended victim to wriggle to safety behind a tombstone. At one point a royalist captain and a roundhead lieutenant climbed into the great yew tree from opposite sides, bumped into one another and subsequently engaged in a display of fencing and arboreal acrobatics so dazzling that large numbers of both sides simply stood and watched in amazement for half an hour.

But the heroine of the hour was Mrs Bibbings, whose cottage overlooked the village square. From her kitchen window she spotted her son Peter and several of his comrades engaged in hand to hand combat outside, whereupon she strode into the fray and bid them stop for refreshment. Ignoring their protestations that they were in the middle of a battle, she declared that the battle could wait and insisted that all the combatants come into the house. Being young lads to a man, tired and hungry, they obeyed, for none dared gainsay the stern maternal command, trooped sheepishly into the kitchen, the parliamentarians following the local boys, and sat down on opposite sides of the long table. After large plates of mutton stew with dumplings, home-baked bread and Repstock cheese washed down with quarts of ale, they simply hadn't the heart to resume fighting and retired to Farmer Frant's barn behind the church to play cards until the battle was over.

Someone must have seen them, for in due course the news of this incident reached the ears of General Wyrecroft. He sensibly decided not to court martial the lads but gave them a severe dressing down and determined to speak his mind to this meddlesome woman who had dared to obstruct His Majesty's troops in the discharge of their duty. Martha Bibbings proved to be a handsome red-headed woman with beguiling hazel eyes, and a widow at that. He found her in animated negotiations with the butcher over the hind-quarters of a deer felled by a stray musket ball - the only recorded casualty of the conflict. Having secured a satisfactory deal, she turned to the general and remarked that it grieved her to see a fine figure of a man in such obvious need of sustenance.

Far from admonishing the good lady, the general found himself momentarily at a loss for words - and then proposing to her just hours later with a bellyful of haunch of venison and port. Theirs was to be both a happy marriage and a highly successful business partnership when the new Lady Wyrecroft took charge of regimental catering. The old adage that an army marches on its stomach was never truer than it was of the Royal Stiltshire Regiment.

Peter Bibbings enjoyed a successful military career, rising swiftly to the rank of lieutenant-colonel. It was even said in high places that he might succeed his step-father as commander of the regiment. But his heart belonged to Goadinger and at the age of 40 he retired from the army, returned to the village and bought his uncle's farm. Later on, as churchwarden, he put forward his plan to raise money by public subscription to build a tower on the hill to commemorate the Goadinger Skirmish. The scheme was generously supported by his fellow landowners, not least three men who were not of local origin; former roundheads all, they had learned to appreciate the simple pleasures in life, settled in Goadinger and married local girls. For them, the tower represented the day they had seen the light over a jug of ale and a bowl of mutton stew.

The Sniblings

A now extinct family, the Sniblings are believed to have been descended from common ancestors with the Snebwoods and were associated with the twin villages of Snibling Magna and Snibling Parva. (The fact that both villages stand on the River Snibb may be no more than a strange coincidence.) Their wealth, accumulated through shipping and porcine husbandry, enabled the building between 1680 and 1730 of Snibling Hall, a splendid mansion which for sheer opulence exceeded even the Marquess of Eyvesborough's Lower Crenton Place.

In 1740 Sir Aloysius Snibling (1694-1763) erected a perfectly spherical folly, carved from a single lump of granite and weighing over 50 tons, on the top of Breen Hill, which overlooks Snibling Magna. There it stood for nearly 30 years, affording splendid views of the surrounding countryside to anyone prepared to enter through a door in the plinth and climb up a narrow shaft through the ball to the viewing hatch on top.

However, during a severe storm one night in the winter of 1769, it toppled from its plinth and began rolling down the well-worn path towards the village. After a mile or so the path veers sharply to the right and the massive ball, now possessed of considerable momentum, continued in a straight line, leaping the bank and remaining airborne for some 120 yards* before it came back to earth and resumed rolling down Upper Snibling Lane, from whence it flattened a beautiful set of wrought iron gates and maintained its relentless progress straight down the grand drive to Snibling Hall. With a fearsome crash the mighty granite sphere burst the columns of the portico asunder, splintered the main door and rumbled through the great hall, demolishing everything in its path. Fortunately, the family bedrooms and servants' quarters were in the east and west wings and miraculously no-one was killed or seriously injured. The great ball bounced off the terraces, cutting a swathe through the south lawn, felled a number of trees in the orchard and continued its downward journey, finally coming to rest in a piece of boggy farmland half a mile from the house, where it has lain half-buried ever since.

Sadly the Hon. Alexander Snibling (son of Sir Aloysius) had squandered most of his late father's fortune and was in no position to repair the devastated mansion. He moved into a small cottage on the estate and Snibling Hall became an imposing ruin. Much of it was demolished for safety reasons in 1830 but parts of the west wing remain to this day.

* This was vividly attested to by a group of terrified farmhands returning from the pub.

Oyker and Smolder

Whereas the villages of Oxbake and Jupton have been engaged in a feud for nearly 600 years, the neighbouring Dongland villages of Oyker and Smolder enjoy a more benign but no less singular relationship. No-one actually knows for certain which village is which and they have swapped names numerous times in the past.

Time was when revenue men or surveyors arriving in, as they thought, Smolder might be told: "Oh no, sir, this be Oyker; Smolder be down the road". On their next visit it might be the other way round. And it had always been that way.

The curious thing is that, although the exchanges of name appear to have happened spontaneously and at random intervals, all the inhabitants of both villages would be in instant and total agreement about the current nomenclature and prepared to vociferously deny that it had ever been any different. Furthermore, such written evidence as there was, mainly signposts and parish records would always confirm the spoken word, much to the confusion of outsiders.

It is impossible to say how often the exchange occurred prior to the 18th century, although there are references to the phenomenon in the ancient chronicles of both St Cedd's College and Flover Priory. It would appear to have occurred in 1458 and 1462 and possibly in 1512. Records for the 17th century are sparse but circumstantial evidence points to a change around 1670. Certainly it happened in 1707 and 1710 and again in 1726.

The Rev'd Seymour Smogg, who, as Rector of nearby Yurch and later Archdeacon of Brinceton, had more than a passing interest in the matter, noted that no fewer than 11 changes occurred during his 50-year ministry: in 1763, 1764, 1781, 1787, 1790, 1792 (twice), 1794, 1797, 1804 and 1811. One might wonder whether as Archdeacon he sought an explanation from the incumbents of the two parishes and indeed he did, on numerous occasions, but they always colluded with the status quo. In 1797 the Rev'd Clement Wax swore upon oath in a consistory court that he was Vicar of Smolder, despite documentary evidence from the Diocesan archives that he had been instituted as Vicar of Oyker the previous year.

In the late 19th century the name changes came to an end, probably because they became untenable (mass literacy, the invention of the camera and the introduction of regular censuses have all been cited as contributory factors). The two villages have retained their current designations since 1862.

Officially, that is… Local youths still occasionally move signs during the night. And older folk, asked for directions, may scratch their heads and say in a slow Dongland drawl: "Well, sir, they *says* this be Oyker, but it be Smolder really". Until next year, or the year after, or the year after that.

St Magg's is a small island, barely a mile long by half a mile wide, lying off the Stiltshire coast about five miles south of Hermington. Geographically it consists of a single hill rising to about 100 feet and covered in coarse moorland vegetation with few trees.

It derives its name from an 11th century monk called Sonorgis but also known by his common name of Magg. Unlike his near contemporary the Blessed Witta, who roamed the length and breadth of the county dispensing blessings and words of wisdom, Sonorgis opted for a solitary existence on the island. He was, however, kindly disposed to pronounce his benediction upon any who made the journey to his abode and numerous miracles of healing were attributed to him. Although he was never officially beatified, the name St Magg's became attached to the island shortly after his death. Around this time too there arose a rumour that Sonorgis had actually been a woman but, since his or her body was never found, it remains a matter for speculation.

The island remained for the most part uninhabited until the 18th century when the fashion for hermits was at its height. Stiltshire hermits, though, tended to eschew the garden grottos offered by wealthy patrons and, following the lead of one Brother Anselm, made their way to St Magg's Island. For a while there were just two of them living amicably at opposite ends of the island but, over the next few years, numbers gradually increased. At one stage there were as many as 34, although a few quickly became disillusioned and left. The fundamental issue of course was that these solitude-seekers became increasingly irked by the close proximity to one another but there were practical problems too.

Firstly, the water supply: the only source of fresh water is a small spring on the west side. Rainwater collects in porous rock at the top of the hill, bubbles up through a small fissure, cascades over a rocky ledge in a diminutive waterfall and runs down a ditch some 30 yards long before disappearing to re-emerge through the roof of a little cave which is only accessible at low tide. While the early settlers had agreed on access to this precious resource, they were reluctant to share it with later arrivals. Some of the latter even set up a primitive desalination plant on the south-east tip of the island. The other big problem was sanitation, for which each hermit made his own arrangements. Add to that the fact that some had brought goats and chickens and it is not difficult to imagine that many parts of the tiny island became very unsavoury indeed.

Matters came to a head when Brother Radegund, who was wont to obtain his drinking water from the cave, became violently ill and accused Brother Leopold of polluting his water supply. Despite a raging fever, he determined to watch Leopold's movements, as it were, and after a day or two caught him in the act of relieving himself in the ditch above the cave, whereupon he repeated the accusation with the utmost vehemence. Incensed at being disturbed in his ablutions, Leopold retaliated and the two quickly came to blows. Other hermits, on hearing the commotion, began to take sides. During the ensuing melee Radegund, weakened by fever and dehydration, suffered heart failure and died.

As a rule, the authorities on the mainland took little notice of what happened on St Magg's Island but, when it became known that a man had died in suspicious circumstances, several officers of the Brobmore Regis Constabulary were sent to investigate. Leopold and 14 other hermits were arrested and charged with causing an affray, for which they were subsequently convicted and sentenced to five years in gaol. Over the next few months, others departed until only Brother Anselm who had started the whole colony was left. And there he stayed, leading a life of simplicity and blissful contemplation, for the remaining 53 years of his life. His death at the age of 97 might have gone unnoticed but for two Flugford fishermen who, intrigued by the presence of an uncommonly large murder of crows, went ashore and discovered Anselm's much-pecked corpse on the beach.

Some 50 years later, a character calling himself Brother James took up residence in a declared attempt to emulate Brother Anselm, although his devotions were aided by regular deliveries of Oxbake Ale – if the words of the eponymous song are to be believed! In 1953 the eccentric nihilistic artist Ivan Lentil took up residence in a flimsy wooden hut on the island, where he died of pneumonia the following winter.

Today St Magg's Island is inhabited only by seabirds, rabbits and a small herd of feral goats, although it remains an attractive destination for some hardy souls wanting to camp under Spartan conditions or simply get away from it all for a few days.

The "M's"

Apart from Gryatt Island the only other offshore islands of any size are Ni'M, Mid'M and Fa'M, stretching out in a line opposite the estuary of the River Tworp. The prefix indicates their relative proximity to the mainland while the "M" is apparently a contraction of the word "holm", which of course means island. All three are uninhabited but are maintained as a nature reserve, being a breeding ground for numerous species of seabird as well as the last remaining habitat of the once-common Dongland shrew. They are also sometimes known as the Goose Islands for reasons which are not at all clear.

Stiltshire, being a maritime county, has had its share of sea-faring heroes, but none quite as illustrious as Saucy Sam the Pirate.

Samuel Tobias Wenton was born in 1698, the son of a clergyman probably at Smitley, and was distantly related to the murdered Rector of Smoatham. Having an academic bent, he graduated from Stangley Hall, where he also excelled at rowing, and subsequently became Professor of Mathematics at St Cedd's.

Around the year 1740 he became involved in a protracted and acrimonious dispute with his opposite number at Old College, Professor Amos Bludge. One May afternoon in 1741 the two men chanced to meet in the middle of Gnashing Bridge. A heated argument quickly turned to blows, Bludge lost his balance and fell over the parapet, splitting his head open on the sharp stones below. Wenton, fearing the worst, fled from Stilchester that night, taking with him little but a brace of pistols and his pet parrot, a scarlet macaw named Pythagoras.

Arriving in Stilhaven, he stowed away on a small merchant ship, the Golden Boar. Discovering that the captain and most of the officers were ashore, he decided to commandeer the vessel. As it turned out, the crew bore little affection for their captain, a cruel and curmudgeonly man, and having taken on supplies of ale, rum and salt pork, were more than happy to put to sea with the jovial Wenton in command.

Thus, Professor Samuel Wenton became a pirate. His modus operandi was to patrol the waters just beyond the shipping lanes into Stilhaven and make occasional incursions under cover of Gryatt Island to ambush outgoing ships and relieve them of their provisions. These encounters seldom resulted in any serious bloodshed but were notable for their audacity and Wenton quickly acquired the nickname of "Saucy Sam".

Lady Genevieve de Pailey was born in 1716, the youngest daughter of the 10th Marquess of Eyvesborough. An attractive and talented young woman, she had studied at Stangley Hall where she made the acquaintance of Samuel Wenton and subsequently formed a clandestine relationship with him. On hearing the news of his departure from the university and subsequent piratical activities, she determined to join her lover. Leaving Lower Crenton Place by night, she rode to Sowport, found a small rowing boat and, risking the treacherous currents, rowed across to Gryatt Island and went straight to the lighthouse.

The lighthouse keeper, Ambrose Bones, was another former Stilchester don who had left the university a few years earlier in pursuit of a simpler life and spent his days, or mostly his nights, tending the light and composing strange aleatoric music with only an owl called Erasmus for company. Genevieve had surmised, correctly, that Wenton was in contact with his former colleague and indeed the two men had devised a sophisticated code of signals whereby Bones kept Wenton informed of shipping movements in and out of the harbour. Within a few days, Sam had been appraised of her presence on the island and came to collect her. The fittings of the captain's cabin were a bit sparse but a couple more raids soon saw it furnished in a manner more befitting a lady.

Of course, the news of her defection scandalised Stiltshire society, but over the following months a number of wives and sweethearts of the Golden Boar's crew made their way to Gryatt Island and joined the ship. Life on board the Golden Boar was by all accounts most convivial, with much good food and wine consumed.

Furthermore, some of the crew, being poorly educated, took the opportunity to improve their literary and especially mathematical skills. Having been taught to recite their tables by Pythagoras the parrot, they would proceed to Genevieve's ingenious exposition of (Euclidean and non-Euclidean) geometry in sailcloth or Sam's practical trigonometry for seafarers and thus became highly adept at calculating the speed and distance of other vessels and trimming their sails accordingly.

From time to time Sam and his crew would sail across to France, barter some prime Stiltshire pork for wine and cheese and enjoy a little Gallic culture. During the winter they would spend a month or three in the Mediterranean or the Canary Islands. But, idyllic though this life must have been, there came a time when Saucy Sam and Genevieve began to yearn for a more settled existence.

Curiously, it was the arrival in 1752 of another pirate ship on the scene which provided the opportunity. Wally Waxbeard was a conventional pirate, an altogether more bloodthirsty character and a thorn in the flesh of the Revenue men. When the Dirty Raven began operating in the area, the Port of Stilhaven Authority offered a substantial bounty for Waxbeard's capture. Sam began to conceive a plan.

Waxbeard, too, was in the habit of plundering ships for provisions when not engaged in more lucrative and murderous raids, but he was operating in unfamiliar territory unlike Sam's crew who knew the Stiltshire and Dongland coastal waters like the backs of their hands (and of course were all outstanding mathematicians). Whenever the Dirty Raven intercepted a merchantman, the Golden Boar had been there first and there was scarcely anything edible or potable to be taken.

After several weeks of this, Waxbeard's men were half starved, their liquor gone, and their spirits of the other kind at a low ebb. One misty morning at daybreak, the Golden Boar glided silently up behind the Dirty Raven. Lowering two small boats, Sam and a few of his trusty comrades rowed noiselessly across to the other ship with coils of well-tarred rope and several kegs of a poor quality but seriously over-proof rum. These they lashed to the Dirty Raven's timbers fore and aft, lit the fuses and beat a hasty retreat. Within minutes the entire ship was ablaze. As the charred remains of the hull sank beneath the waves, the Golden Boar returned to the scene where Waxbeard, his trademark whiskers somewhat charred, was found clinging to a broken spar and quickly taken into custody. Others who tried to climb aboard were repelled with a heavy boot and the helpful advice that "St Enoch's Head be just a couple o' leagues that-a-way".

The ship sailed swiftly to Hakeford where, under cover of darkness, a messenger was despatched to convey Sam's terms to the authorities in Stilhaven - the delivery of Waxbeard in return for an unconditional pardon for Sam and his crew. Now Sam's crimes were as nothing compared to those of Waxbeard, so the deal was accepted and the High Sheriff of Stiltshire signed the warrant, albeit with a certain reluctance since only three months earlier a shipment of claret bound for his own cellars had found its way on to Sam's table.

The Golden Boar was moored in Stilhaven harbour and became a floating tavern, run by Sam and Genevieve with many of the former crew helping out behind the bar or just popping in for a drink. Among the first customers was Genevieve's brother, Exeter de Pailey, who had succeeded to the Marquessate some five years earlier and secretly admired his sister's adventurous spirit (sadly, their father never forgave her and disinherited her on his deathbed). The pub became enormously popular, but folk would grumble that it was never open at Christmastide - in fact it wasn't even there but hosting a party somewhere in warmer waters.

The Rev'd Sidney Otter

The renowned naturalist was born in 1769, studied at Flover and in 1795 became Rector of Thrimp, where he remained until his death in 1848.

Like most clergymen of the time, Sidney Otter was a man of great intellect, desirous of spending his time in worthy scholarly pursuits. Compared with many of his contemporaries, he was at a considerable disadvantage insofar as the living of a tiny parish like Thrimp did not afford him the luxury of a curate to whom he could delegate tiresome tasks such as conducting services and visiting the sick.

Being a logical and resourceful man, he set about improving his lot by performing what might in these enlightened days be called a time and motion study or a quality assurance management audit or some such expression. Visiting the sick, he decided, was not a major drain upon his resources, Thrimp being a village of a mere 71 souls and most of them housed in fairly hardy bodies. With regard to the conduct of divine service, prayer was not an expendable item but could be kept to a minimum, readings from scripture were laid down in the lectionary and he enjoyed singing hymns and psalms. In the final analysis, the activities which made the most unreasonable demands upon his time were the composition and delivery of sermons.

Fortunately, during his days as a theological student and a young curate he had painstakingly written down all his sermons and kept all but the very worst of them, so he now had a collection of 579, catering for every season of the liturgical calendar and covering almost every theological topic of any significance. These he had published in a book, copies of which were placed in the pews alongside the hymnals and prayer books. Thus, at the appropriate point in the service, the Rector could announce "Sermon number 165" and then leave the congregation to read it while he slipped out of the church to perform some more pressing task such as setting a broken bat's wing, collecting the honey from his hives or feeding his Venus fly traps.

The system was not without its teething troubles. Once, during Matins, he became so engrossed in whatever he was doing that he forgot to return to the church until three hours later when he found the congregation still sitting there waiting for the final hymn and blessing, some having fallen asleep from sheer boredom and others becoming increasingly agitated at the thought of the Sunday joint gradually incinerating in the oven at home. This problem was countered by moving the sermon to the end of the service. Then, lest anyone should be tempted to devote insufficient time to it or, Heaven forbid, to leave the church without reading the sermon at all, he adopted the practice of stopping people at random in the street during the week and asking questions.

Needless to say, the answers often left much to be desired. Folk would read the wrong sermon, or their minds would go back to the previous week or get confused between Matins and Evensong. On one occasion the Bishop made a visitation and, having ascertained that the previous week's sermon had been on the theme of stewardship, asked a young boy what the Rector would like to see on the plate. The lad looked thoughtful for a moment and then replied: "the head of John the Baptist?".

Despite his slightly cavalier attitude to their spiritual welfare, the Rev'd Otter was much loved by his parishioners. When he died there was a week-long wake in the village inn, which later changed its name to the Capsicum in remembrance of his fondness for growing exotic vegetables. Nearly a century later his successor-but-four, the Rev'd Ezra Rhodes, turned part of the rambling rectory into a museum dedicated to his illustrious predecessor.

[Ezra Rhodes was himself a noted scholar and historian; the Museum of Stiltshire Lore in Stilchester is named after him.]

The industrial revolution came slowly to Stiltshire. The county's foremost industry is the production of sieves and colanders which has taken place in the small town of Narkington since the 15th century. The most celebrated master Sievewright was Simeon Olquire the second (1749-1828), founder of the firm Treen and Olquire and largely responsible for the rebuilding of the Sievewrights Hall in Stilchester in its current form.

One of Stiltshire's most unusual artefacts may be seen in the Hall - the 18th century ballot box of The Worshipful Company of Sievewrights. Superficially, the brass-bound mahogany box is not unlike those used by other ancient societies for secret ballots. Members cast their votes by putting their hands through a hole in the top and dropping balls into drawers marked 'aye' or 'nay'. What makes the Sievewrights' box unique is the clockwork shutter mechanism designed by the celebrated locksmith Elijah Shunhose (1691-1758). The voter pulls a lever to activate the clockwork and then has 5 seconds to cast his vote before a well-honed steel blade springs across the hand hole and closes the box. Sievewrights voting for the first time were customarily invited to test the efficacy of the mechanism by inserting a carrot into the orifice.

Around three hundred years ago, it was tacitly accepted that members might try to re-distribute the votes providing their hands were not in the box for an unseemly length of time; indeed, it was for this reason that senior officers traditionally cast their votes last. Eventually the practice became so blatant that the five second rule was introduced and subsequently enforced by Shunhose's mechanism. However, by Victorian times any hint of ballot-rigging would have been regarded as gross impropriety and members would frequently demonstrate their probity by setting the shutter to activate in just 2 or 3 seconds. For a while, missing fingertips were regarded almost as a badge of honour, until the resulting loss of manual dexterity became such a problem among sievewrights that the blade was fitted with a rubber shield. The ivory balls still bear the bloodstains to this day.

In the early 18th century the land around the villages of East and West Pawtley was found to be rich in high quality chalk and a type of limestone well suited to building. Several quarries were opened and continued to supply both chalk and stone for nearly two centuries, reaching their heyday under the ownership of George Mugg (1830 to 1911). Eventually the business folded due to falling demand and the declining quality of the remaining deposits, but workers' families had swelled the population of East Pawtley to the extent that a new church was required, so Saint Jude's was built in one of the abandoned quarries. The local football team is known as the Pawtley Muggs.

Another centre of light industry is Gruntlington with a thriving trade in paper making and printing and later the manufacture of small vehicles including the famous *Rumbler* motorcycles. It is also the home of the confectioners Gruntlington Sugarsmiths, makers of Dr John's Chalky Mints, Beer Humbugs, Clove Snakes and Chorister's Choice, the ultimate "little black things" beloved of generations of singers. As befits an industrial town, Gruntlington has a thriving brass band; its signature tune, the Gruntlington Post, was written by the local composer George Crumbleforth (later Sir George).

The county's first canal, a mere 3 miles in length, was built for the sieve industry in 1740 and connects the centre of Narkington with the river near Stiltford. But it was Sir Reuben Gullett (1721-1800), "the father of Stiltshire navigation", who really put artificial waterways on the map. A graduate of Stangley hall where he studied music* as well as physics, he was quick to grasp the possibilities of inland water-borne transportation.

His first project was the Mid-Stilts Canal, built to carry stone from the newly opened Pawtley quarries to the river Stilt and opened in 1754. Spanning 26 miles of fairly flat open country with just 16 locks, it was built quickly and was soon carrying enough freight and livestock to ensure a handsome return for its investors. The only problem was the tendency of pigs to jump out of the low and slow-moving narrow boats while passing through Bayconhurst Woods during the pannage season.

Next came the Stiltford and Eyvesborough Canal, a much more ambitious project given the hilly terrain; it includes a flight of 25 locks (with five pubs at regular intervals) at Fletley and the long, haunted Beards Warden tunnel. Notwithstanding the technical difficulties, its success was sufficient to ensure Gullett's knighthood.

Finally came the Chineham and Prokeworth Canal, 43 miles long, linking those towns with Stilchester and Stilhaven. Barely predating the railway age, it was never a great success commercially and fell into disuse at the beginning of the 20th century.

Today of course the canals are much used for recreational purposes as well as still supporting a small amount of trade. The "Stiltshire King" can be completed in a week and entails boating north up the river from Stilchester to Stiltford then taking the Stiltford and Eyvesborough Canal to Twixham Market, the river Eyve to Pawtley, and the Mid-Stilts to Stoulton-by-Stilt, returning by the river to Stilchester. Since the recent reopening of the Chineham and Prokeworth, navigating the "Stiltshire Great Ring" has become a possibility for those with three weeks or so to spare.

* Gullett is still remembered not just as a civil engineer but as an outstanding bassoonist and composer of Anglican chant.

The Thrice-Wessleys

In 1739 Josiah Wessley (1712-69), the son of a moderately prosperous pig farmer, married Emelia Rice, a daughter of the wealthy family who dominated the Gruntlington printing trade, and changed his name to Rice-Wessley. A generation later, Greville (1742-1801) married Alma Rice and changed the family name again to Rice-Rice-Wessley. When his son Gervais (1773-1851) married Cynthia Rice, he decided that Rice-Rice-Rice-Wessley was too cumbersome and adopted the name Thrice-Wessley instead. The elders of the Rice clan were not pleased but, since the Wessleys had by then assimilated a large proportion of the Rice fortune and there were no more daughters or dowries immediately forthcoming, noses were gently thumbed and the new name remained.

They lived at Horbold Hall. St Anthony's church, Horbold, a magnificent edifice albeit ridiculously large for the tiny village, was built through the generosity of Gervais and his son, the Hon. Hertford Thrice-Wessley (1811-88), MP for Lonchelsea. The latter, probably the most eccentric of the dynasty, also built the folly on Horbold Hill, a curious structure consisting of a round tower surmounted by an octagonal belfry with eight prominent gargoyles and a large weathervane.

His grandson Sebastian Thrice-Wessley (1887-1928), an actor and noted bon viveur, was educated at Stilchester Academy and St Cedd's College, where his thespian tendencies first began to emerge. He performed on the West End stage from time to time and more frequently at local venues such as the Eyvesborough Playhouse, the Elysium, Apstrow, and the Arcadia, Brobmore Regis. His last appearance was as the lead in "The Irrelevance of being Luke Warm" by the Stiltshire playwright, Guy Thame.

The Stiltmouth Floating Railway

It was in the year 1870, that the Stilhaven Corporation decided that a crossing of the Stilt estuary would be good for commerce and tourism. The distinguished civil engineer, Hector Fostlethwaite, was engaged to devise a suitable solution to the problem. In his considered opinion, the distance between the hamlet of Stiltmouth on the west bank and the village of Sowport on the eastern side was too great, and the clearance required by the tall-masted ships of the day too high, to admit the construction of a bridge by any then known technique. However, having surveyed the sea bed between these two points he concluded that its contours were smooth enough to accommodate the novel solution of a submerged railway.

Initially the idea had been for a totally submersible train but when the current lack of expertise in the building of pressurised vehicles became all too apparent, he hit upon an even more novel solution: a railway track would be laid upon the sea bed and the rolling stock would be manufactured in two parts. The lower portion of each carriage consisted of two four-wheeled bogies, each with a long vertical pole projecting upwards from its centre, surrounded at the bottom by a fat rubber grommet. The upper portion resembled a flat-bottomed boat having in its midst two water-tight vertical tubes to accommodate the aforementioned poles. When the train was on land, the carriages would sit upon the rubber grommets with the poles projecting skyward; as it ventured into the water, the upper portion of the carriage would float up the pole, thus keeping the passengers dry whilst moving with the undercarriage as it progressed along the sea bed.

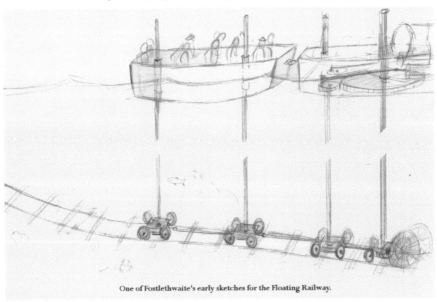

One of Fostlethwaite's early sketches for the Floating Railway.

The locomotive was of similar construction, having additionally a splined vertical drive shaft around which fitted a sliding cog enmeshed with a large horizontal fly wheel driven by a steam engine. Thus, as the vessel rose higher in the water the steam engine was still able to provide traction to the driving wheels below via the splined shaft and a system of bevelled gears. After the initial testing with the engine pulling then pushing the train, it transpired that the ideal configuration was to place the locomotive in the centre with three carriages fore and aft.

The Floating Railway was inaugurated on the 6th June 1873 in the presence of the Mayor of Stilhaven and the Marquess of Eyvesborough. With Mr Fostlethwaite and the crew in the locomotive, the driver sounded a long triumphal toot on the whistle, engaged gear and the train lurched forward into the estuary. Some 12 minutes later it arrived safely in Sowport to the cheers of numerous bystanders. After a short respite the driver engaged reverse gear and the train lumbered slowly back to Stiltmouth, whereupon the Mayor and assorted dignitaries boarded the carriages with some trepidation and were conveyed eastwards and then westwards again without mishap.

For several months the Floating Railway plied back and forth across the estuary for a fare of 3d single or 5d return and was deemed to be a great success. Come November, however, there had been much rain in the hills north of the county and the Stilt was flowing at somewhat higher capacity than normal. The 9.30 train from Sowport having reached the middle of its course, it became apparent that the strength of the current was tending to sweep the train seaward. All of a sudden, the poles of the carriages began to tilt alarmingly and within seconds all the carriages had slipped off the poles entirely and were soon being born out to sea on the strong rip tide. When the train failed to arrive on schedule, the Station Master at Stiltmouth raised the alarm and the Stilhaven lifeboat was launched in pursuit of the errant train. Fortunately, however, it came to rest on the shore at Gryatt Island without loss of life or limb.

This unfortunate incident prompted Fostlethwaite to consider a major re-design of the rolling stock and the railway was out of service for some weeks while ballast weights were added to the bogies to add stability and the tops of the poles were capped to prevent the carriages floating free again. These changes proved successful and the railway ran regularly without incident for a further year or so. Then one morning in March 1875, the 11.00 from Stiltmouth ran into a spot of bother.

Approaching the middle of the channel, the driver became aware that passengers in the front carriage were becoming more than a little agitated and perceived the reason to be that that carriage was awash with water. He immediately applied the brakes but by the time the train came to rest, all three leading carriages were semi-submerged and the passengers frantically scrambling towards the rear of the train.

Unfortunately, the weight of numerous bodies passing through the locomotive caused it to dip below the water line, at which point water entered the fire box, extinguishing the flames in a great hiss of steam.

The driver and fireman swiftly uncoupled the loco which, being by far the heaviest part of the train, promptly vanished beneath the waves as the two men were helped into the adjoining carriage. Fortunately, a collier bound for Stilhaven passed by the scene only a few minutes later and the crew were able to rescue the frantic passengers clinging desperately to the tops of the poles which were now barely above water level.

Fostlethwaite, having been appraised of the disaster, hurried to Stilhaven to be met by the Harbour Master brandishing a set of tide tables. It appears he had neglected to take the spring tide into account when calculating the length of the poles.

This time the problems proved more intractable. The train was immobilised on the sea bed in the middle of the estuary; to recover it would require divers to attach cables so that the carriages could be winched ashore. Meanwhile, its poles constituted a serious danger to shipping. By the time the divers could be mobilised, the gears had already begun to rust and moving the stricken vehicle proved no easy task so they were ordered instead to saw off the poles.

Meanwhile, searching questions were being asked in the council chamber and the local press. It emerged that the railway had been running at a loss for some time, not least because once the novelty had worn off there were not actually many people who wanted to travel from Stiltmouth to Sowport on a daily basis. Before the salvage operation could be completed, the Floating Railway Company had been declared bankrupt. Fostlethwaite had left the county in disgrace, his hopes of a knighthood dashed and his career in ruins.

The station buildings at Stiltmouth still stand, although those on the Sowport side have long since become part of the sprat market. The rolling stock was eventually recovered by a private salvage firm in the 1920s and one well corroded carriage bought by a local eccentric can still be seen in a boat yard on Stilhaven Harbour. A plan to use the rails to launch the new Sowport lifeboat in the 1950s came to nothing and they still lie upon the sea bed, a rusting reminder of one of the most ingenious but absurdly impractical feats of engineering ever undertaken.

The Burnthrope Pentacycle

Horace Burnthrope was born in St Hilda's just outside Eyvesborough in 1855. Little is known of his early life apart from the fact that even as a young boy he had a fascination with mechanical devices. At the age of eight, he acquired a degree of local notoriety when he accidentally knocked the weathercock off the parish church with a giant catapult of his own construction.

Shortly afterwards he acquired a small steam engine which he determined to restore and improve upon. An inventive genius was nearly extinguished in its prime when the boiler exploded and scalded him badly, causing a permanent disfigurement which led to his acquiring the nickname "Bogey Burnthrope" later in life. Undeterred, he then attached two paddle steamer type wheels to the engine, mounted it on a small raft and harnessed it to a horse which he stood in the stream with the intention of demonstrating by means of a tug o' war whether beast or machine was the more powerful. It soon became clear that the result was a decisive victory for the former, for immediately upon the engine being started the horse took fright and ran amok through the village, dragging the hissing, clanking machine behind it. Eventually it bolted into the smithy, where the blacksmith managed to restrain the terrified animal and silenced the engine for ever with a mighty blow from his hammer.

Horace was briefly apprenticed to a pyrotechnist in Eyvesborough, and might have had a promising career in fireworks, for the lad had a rich imagination and was not afraid to try out new techniques, despite his limited knowledge. His only mistake was to use his employer's compost heap as a test bed for his latest creation and to miscalculate the amount of gunpowder by a factor of ten. Several cubic yards of well-rotted compost recently enriched by the addition of some fresh manure were blown skyward and descended over a radius of about 200 yards. His popularity with the good people of Dovegardens was not enhanced by the fact that this incident occurred on a Monday which of course, in those days, was universally regarded as washing day.

But it was locomotion that was always his greatest love, and the invention of the internal combustion engine opened up a whole new world of possibilities for the young Horace. In 1892, he rented a factory in Gruntlington to manufacture motorised tricycles. The venture met with a modicum of success, and a number of his sturdy little three wheelers were to be seen puttering around the roads of Stiltshire in the early years of the 20th century.

Always at the forefront of technical innovation, and never one to rest on his laurels, Horace eventually became convinced that five was the optimum number of wheels for a motorised vehicle. He patented a complicated suspension system based on cantilever arms and coil springs and in the Autumn of 1908 the "Burnthrope

Pentacycle" went into production. It was a strange looking machine with an enormous central wheel driven by a single cylinder engine at the rear. Four smaller wheels extended from the chassis on spindly legs, the front two being steered by the driver who sat forward of and to the right of the central wheel. One passenger sat on the driver's left, and two others at the rear facing outwards at an angle of 45 degrees. The first customer was the 16th Marquess of Eyvesborough, an adventurous gentleman with a penchant for new-fangled devices. Pentacycle No. 1 was rolled out of the factory to the accompaniment of a spirited fanfare from the Gruntlington brass band and a speech by the Mayor, before being ceremoniously handed over to his Lordship who donned his goggles and mounted the contraption and drove off with a wave of his cap to the assembled crowd.

A few days later, the honourable gentleman, whilst putting the machine through its paces, drove it at some speed over the Prumeford Bridge. Upon reaching the apogee of that ancient and somewhat convex structure, the Pentacycle suffered a grave mechanical failure when a crucial weld gave way, whereupon the offside right cantilever arm suddenly and vigorously contracted, flinging the driving seat, with his lordship upon it, over the parapet of the bridge. Fortunately, the Marquess narrowly missed being pitched head first on one of the stone piers and landed on his backside in a bed of reeds. Being of a kindly and more than averagely sporting disposition, he declined to sue Burnthrope but merely returned the wreckage of the machine, demanded a refund and wished him better luck next time.

About six months later, the Pentacycle mark II, with much modified suspension, was complete. This time, rather than take any advance orders, Horace decided to test it rigorously himself. Initial trials having proved encouraging, he decided to put it to the ultimate test and drove at full throttle over the Prumeford Bridge. Behaving quite differently to its predecessor, the mark II, keeping all its joints intact, leapt a full six feet in the air from the summit of the bridge. As the wheels left the ground, the springs contracted, drawing the legs in under the body and the machine skipped down the road, finally coming to rest in a gateway looking like a partially drowned spider. At this point, a reporter from the Gruntlington Herald who happened to be passing but knew a good story when he saw one, stopped and scribbled some notes which became the basis of an article with the headline "Burnthrope Buggy Bust Again" in the following Friday's edition.

Sadly, Burnthrope never sold another Pentacycle, his credibility as provider of safe and reliable transport having been completely shattered. Eventually, he was forced to sell his factory and rent a smallholding with a large shed where he repaired agricultural machinery and built ingenious theatrical props. But he never gave up his dream and spent most of his spare time seeking to improve the suspension, never wavering in his belief in the power of five wheeled locomotion and confident that one day Pentacycles would be as common a sight on the street as the horse and cart.

Horace Burnthrope died in 1935 and the manner of his passing was as eccentric as many an episode in his life. He was driving the Pentacycle Mk 43 westwards along the road from Eyvesborough to Prumeford when he suffered a seizure. With his foot pressing heavily upon the accelerator pedal, the machine proceeded along the High Street at full throttle and sailed gracefully over the Prumeford Bridge with the merest hint of a bounce and all five wheels firmly on the road. This phenomenon was observed by at least half a dozen people who waved and cheered loudly at Horace, not realising that he was dead. Whatever miraculous improvement he had made to the suspension in his final weeks, we shall never know, for half a mile further on, where the road bends sharply to the right, the Pentacycle continued straight ahead into a brick wall, its inventor's corpse sitting unscathed in the driving seat but the finer details of its mechanical arms reduced to a heap of twisted metal.

The Great Custardo

Stiltshire's best loved music hall entertainer was born George Grout, a coalman's son, at Crachelton-on-Sea in 1874. As a young boy he possessed a naturally comical appearance, with a large nose and ears and ginger hair, and an inventive sense of humour. One day when the Punch and Judy man failed to turn up at his accustomed hour on the beach, young George improvised his own puppet show behind a breakwater, using only pebbles and pieces of driftwood. He had also developed the art of making farting noises with his armpit to the extent that he could produce a plausible rendering of the National Anthem or Brahms' Lullaby.

On leaving school he went to work in a bakery but continued to put on amateur entertainments for the amusement of local people - until he was spotted by a talent scout from the Stilhaven Music Hall. He had already acquired the nickname Custardo following an accident with a batch of custard pies in the bakery but on the billboards it was prefixed by "The Great" and the name stuck.

For more than 50 years he entertained audiences in the music halls and theatres as well as giving matinee performances on the piers at Brobmore Regis, Crachelton-on-Sea and Lonchelsea, with his trademark purple bowler hat, oversized shoes and baggy trousers which frequently fell down, only to be magically reinstated with a tweak of his bulbous red nose. He died of a stroke just hours after his last performance in the Pavilion at his home town.

Cuggley Grange

Digby Smallpot (1865-1952) grew up on his father's estate at Cuggley. As a boy he exhibited a scientific curiosity and a concern for the natural world which was to lead him to become a conservationist decades before that became a recognisable, let alone fashionable, activity. After graduating from St Cedd's he started his own architectural practice in Stilhaven, designing modest cottages with insulated walls, windmill-powered dynamos and kitchen gardens aimed at making the occupants largely self-sufficient. On the death of his father in 1908 he inherited the family seat and a small fortune which he invested in fulfilling his dream of a truly energy-efficient community.

Cuggley Grange was a self-contained estate of 36 tall, narrow, energy-conserving houses built on a swamp outside the village. Each house was typically five or six storeys high with one room per floor (on the basis that heat rises) and centrally heated by burning briquettes of pig manure and charcoal. Electricity came from three windmills on a seaward-facing hilltop (which were also capable of grinding corn) and fresh water from underground springs. Sewage was directed into a sealed-off area of the swamp from which methane could be extracted to supplement the solid fuel. The estate had its own farm, bakery, shop and a small brewery and tap-room.

The Composer and the Aviatrix

One of the first residents of Cuggley Grange was the composer Sir George Crumbleforth (1844-1928), best known for his light operettas written in collaboration with the satirical lyricist Sidney Antrobus Pillion. Following the death of his first wife in 1915, he accepted an invitation from Smallpot, a long-standing friend, to try one of the novel energy-conserving dwellings. However, one feature of the tall, thin house was not to his liking: the tiny bathroom which only permitted space for a continental-style hip bath. Accordingly, he arranged for a full-sized luxury enamel bath to be cantilevered out through the south wall of the top storey, fitted with a roll-back canopy and supplied with (manure-powered) hot water.

On the 10th of August 1921 Sir George was taking his morning bath, having opened the canopy to take advantage of the sunshine, when he was seen by the aviatrix Pamela Hock-Martenshawe, who had just taken off from Rimpleham aerodrome in her biplane. Upon landing, Miss Hock-Martenshawe made a complaint to the police, as a result of which Sir George was arrested and brought to trial in Stilhaven Crown Court on a charge of indecent exposure.

Mr Justice Shedham, dismissing the case, famously remarked "a gentleman bathing in what he believes to be the privacy of his own home cannot reasonably be expected to foresee the need to conceal his person from a passing woman in a flying machine."

Here events took a bizarre turn for, on leaving the courtroom, Sir George graciously extended to his accuser an invitation to join him for dinner. She, after some hesitation, accepted and subsequently, notwithstanding the 38-year discrepancy in their ages, became his second wife. Thereafter the new Lady Crumbleforth was frequently to be seen besporting herself in the rooftop bathtub, much to the amusement of her colleagues in the Rimpleham Flying Club.

There is a strange postscript to this story. Most of the Cuggley Grange houses were demolished during the Second World War, including Crumbleforth's. In 2002 the industrial archaeologist Professor David Lunch discovered a bathtub in the swamp which he asserted was the one belonging to Sir George. His colleague Professor Rupert Medlar was sceptical, given Lunch's previous track record* and his assertion the it was "just a bog-standard bath" seemed to be justified when a local resident came forward to claim it. Fred Breeze insisted that the bath once belonged to his parents' house in Claw Lane about 200 yards away. One evening in 1938 his father sent him and his brother Sid to fetch coal in it but, on the return journey, Sid slipped and the two boys let go of the heavy bath which rolled down a bank and quickly sank into the bog.

However, the story took a bizarre twist after an Australian reader spotted a report in the online journal "On Stilts" and showed it to his father. Dan Hammock grew up in Cuggley and emigrated to Adelaide in the 1950s. In 1928 he was apprenticed to a local builder and helped to dismantle the Crumbleforth external bathroom after the composer's death. He recalled that most of the fittings went to a scrap metal merchant but that the bathtub itself was cleaned up and sold to a local man called Breeze for 15 shillings.

This meant of course that Crumbleforth's bath and the coal-laden tub which Fred Breeze and his brother dropped into the bog ten years later were undoubtedly one and the same. Professor Lunch was understandably overjoyed at the news, feeling "exhilarated and exonerated". Mr Breeze donated the tub to the Cuggley Grange museum and it was subsequently reinstalled in one of the three surviving houses.

* Lunch had earlier claimed to have solved the mystery of the Horace Burnthrope's final modifications to the suspension of the Pentacycle, following the discovery of a severely corroded mechanism in the River Prume by two local schoolboys; it later turned out to be a domestic mincer.

The history of Stiltshire is littered with visionaries whose ideas ranged from the inspired to the downright bizarre. In the latter category are a few whose brainchildren actually made it into production. But if you thought the Floating Railway was a crazy idea or that Horace Burnthrope was off his trolley, spare a thought for Stiltshire's least successful inventor.

Robert Bristol Briskett (1888-1967), a gentleman of private means who had graduated from Stangley Hall with a third in physics, first produced a number of designs for unconventional sieves and colanders, all of which he submitted to Treen and Olquire of Narkington for their consideration and all of which were politely rejected. He then turned his attention to railways.

Now Briskett himself was a frequent traveller by train and hated sitting with his back to the engine – indeed, true to his family motto "Never look back", he hated travelling anywhere without being able to see where he was going – hence his revolutionary design started from the premise that every passenger should have an uninterrupted view of the way ahead.

The end result was a vehicle almost 500 feet wide and barely 10 feet long. It consisted of nine interconnected carriages, each running on its own pair of 12-foot-guage rails. At the front of each carriage was a row of seats facing large windows and behind that another row placed 18 inches higher, so that the occupants could see over the heads of those in front. Behind the seats, a corridor ran the entire width of the train with a door at each end, and in the space at the back were small compartments that served variously as lavatories, luggage space and catering facilities. The whole thing was propelled from behind by three small steam locomotives running on tracks 2, 5 and 8.

When Briskett's detailed plans, which had been six years in the making, were submitted to the Railways Board, the response was less than encouraging: "Whilst the construction of the proposed vehicle is within the bounds of possibility, we foresee intractable difficulties in the acquisition of a level, 1000 feet wide strip of land (assuming trains are to run in both directions), not to mention the excessive cost of steel for the provision of 18 sets of rails where two would normally suffice. We are also concerned by the time constraints raised by several hundred passengers boarding or alighting in single file. Furthermore, the inventor appears not to have considered the means of turning the train round at the terminus."

Initially Briskett was devastated by this rejection but after an extended sabbatical in the Faroe Islands he returned to the drawing board. His second design, some four years later, consisted of a single carriage 50 feet square and 20 feet high with an enormous sloping window at the front and the seats arranged in tiers as in a cinema. This required only two sets of rails, was powered by diesel engines under the seating and could be turned around on a fairly tight loop of track. The Board's response was sympathetic to his "strenuous efforts towards saving on space and materials, compared with the previous design" but concluded that "in view of the impracticality of constructing tunnels or bridges on the scale required, we regret we must reject the proposal".

After a seven-year retreat on a Himalayan yak farm, Briskett produced his third design. It was a rehash of the original but this time the passenger compartments comprised a single carriage mounted on a turntable carried by a massive bogey running on a single pair of rails. Where space permitted the carriage – a mere 400 feet wide with three rows of seats - was swivelled to face forwards, the weight of the extremities supported by pneumatic-tyred wheels on telescopic legs. Otherwise it could be aligned parallel to the rails and supported by flanged wheels on a second set of retractable legs, thus enabling it to pass through tunnels and over bridges. The locomotive ran some distance ahead to allow for the swivelling of the carriage which it pulled by means of stout cables. Briskett's submission to the Railways Board was accompanied by a letter expressing regret that his original premise had been somewhat compromised. The reply, by return of post, informed him that "the whole thing is just too damned silly to merit further consideration".

Lesser men may have admitted defeat at this juncture. But after six months in a tent on St Magg's Island, with weekly deliveries of supplies by Flugford fishermen, Briskett came up with yet another idea. The carriage, this time just 300 feet long, was to be hinged at the front so that it could be raised vertically for optimum viewing or lowered to the horizontal for boarding and alighting or negotiating tunnels, the seats swivelling like those of a ferris wheel to keep the occupants upright. He might have submitted this plan but for a chance conversation in the pub with a sewer engineer who pointed out that raising the carriage would require either an immensely powerful hydraulic ram or a complex system of gears and an inordinate amount of time.

Following a flash of inspiration during the next pint, he modified the design to pivot the carriage in the middle. Now the mechanically minded among you will realise that, whilst this does indeed reduce the energy required to rotate the carriage to a negligible amount, it does necessitate the carriage being at least half its own length above the tracks. Nevertheless, it was in this form that Briskett submitted his plans, seemingly oblivious to the fact that previous objections regarding the size of tunnels once again applied, not to mention the inconvenience to passengers of having to climb a 150 foot ladder to take their seats. The reply was again swift and consisted of a photograph of a wastepaper bin.

At this point Briskett lost interest in railways and spent most of the rest of his life attempting to devise a teapot for use in zero-gravity conditions.

Wing Commander "Perry" Dalton-Stool

Arthur Perivale Dalton-Stool was born at Stiltford in 1889, the younger son of Major Reginald Dalton-Stool. Commonly known as "Perry" from an early age, he was educated at the Stilchester Academy and Stangley Hall. While his elder brother Ralph followed in their father's footstep and went on to a highly successful military career, young Perry was fascinated with aviation and learned to fly at the newly-founded Stiltford aerodrome while still an undergraduate.

At the outbreak of WW1 he signed up for the Stiltshire branch of the Royal Flying Corps and quickly became its most competent and audacious pilot. Like many of those early flying aces he cultivated an impressive handlebar moustache; by the end of the war it measured 21 inches from tip to tip. At charity galas society ladies would pay serious money for the privilege of stroking it.

When Stiltford aerodrome became a commercial airport under the auspices of Stilchester Airways in 1926, Perry became their chief pilot, flying small airliners on domestic flights as well as teaching others to fly.

During WW2 he volunteered for service in the RAF, where his skills as a fighter pilot and trainer were much in demand. And he was still flying from Stiltford airfield which had once again become a military airbase. By this time his famous moustache had grown to an incredible 28 inches.

One night in November 1941 he returned from a sortie over France with his port engine on fire but was able to make an emergency landing at Rimpleham aerodrome. The plane came to rest with its undercarriage crippled and both engines now ablaze and flames licking around his feet. By the time Perry opened the cockpit the fire crew were on hand and urging him to jump before the fuel tanks exploded. But he insisted they spray water on his moustache first, lest it should be set on fire as he jumped through the wall of flames. In the event he suffered severe burns to his legs but kept his magnificent whiskers intact.

At the end of the war, Stiltford reverted to being a commercial airport and Perry continued to fly for the next two decades. His mischievous sense of humour nearly cost him his job on one occasion when he stood in the cockpit dressed as the grim reaper while passengers were boarding.

During the severe winter of 1947, Stiltford was effectively isolated by snow drifts to the extent that Perry's local, the Warthog, ran out of beer as Oxbake Brewery had been unable to deliver for a fortnight. Determined to rectify the situation, Perry made his way to the ancient biplane which he kept at Stiltford Airport, took off in a blizzard and flew to Oxbake. The best substitute for a landing strip turned out to be a straight stretch of the Oxbake Canal which was frozen over. Reasoning that, should the ice break, the water was only a few feet deep, he carefully brought the plane down and skidded to a halt just 100 yards from the brewery. Fortunately the ice held and he was able to load the plane with three firkins of porter and several crates of barley wine before returning to Stiltford, much to the relief of his drinking companions.

While his brother, now Lt. Col. Ralph Dalton-Stool CBE, had long since retired with full military honours and devoted his later years to gardening, becoming the founder and first president of the Stiltford Horticultural Society, Perry continued to fly. At the age of 80 he was still flying pleasure trips and introducing the next generation to the pleasures of aviation. And he kept that splendid moustache to the last – when he died in 1978, his coffin was built on a cruciform pattern to accommodate it.

Perry never married – the only love of his life died in tragic circumstances…

Darcey Squeak

Born in 1902, Darcey Squeak trained as a classical ballet dancer but, driven by her wild imagination and the modernising spirit of the 1920s, developed an original style which quickly established her as one of the most popular and highly-paid dancers of her time. Performances of her solo routine, accompanied by her own five-piece band, were invariably sold out.

One of the few props she used was a long and expensive string of pearls which at one point in her act she would spin round her neck like a hula hoop while pirouetting on one foot. On two or three occasions the cord in the necklace snapped and, having lost several of the smaller pearls in this manner, she had the necklace rethreaded on a steel wire. This proved to be a fatal mistake.

On the night of 19th August 1931 Miss Squeak was staying at the Grand Hotel in Brobmore Regis when a fire broke out in the building. Her room was on the first floor at the back, overlooking the Pleasure Gardens. A conveniently-placed gas lamp revealed a flower bed below and no doubt convinced her that this was the best means of escape. She opened the window, snatched the necklace from the dressing table, flinging it around her neck, and jumped. The lamp-post was of the familiar cast iron type with two brackets below the lantern for the lamplighter to rest his ladder upon. The necklace snagged on one of these appendages, the wire held and Darcey was left hanging. No-one saw it happen, since there was a great commotion at the front of the hotel, and within minutes she was dead. She had become engaged to Perry Dalton-Stool just a few days earlier.

The Golden Arm

One of Stiltshire's most outstanding sportsmen was Spencer Arlington Gibbon (1842-88). He first demonstrated his prowess at rowing while at the Stilchester Academy and went on to be stroke for the Stangley Hall eight during a period in which they won the Town and Gown Boat Race an unprecedented 13 times in succession (1859-71).

After serving with the army in India, he returned to Stilchester as Professor of Natural Sciences at St Cedd's and also served as MP for Prume and Pebb from 1874-80. Sadly his life came to an abrupt end when he became the third victim of the acid bath murderer in 1888.

A solid gold cast of Spencer's left forearm, made at the height of his rowing career, has been described by Beef's Auction House as the singular most valuable artefact in the county.

Several of his descendants are well-known. The Rev'd Galadriel Gibbon was the first woman to be ordained priest in the county and is now Archdeacon of Spruntley. Her sister Ariel married the MD of Swallow's Brewery, becoming Lady Ariel when Sir Dudley Swallow received his knighthood. Galadriel's daughter Rebecca Gibbon is the lead singer of the folk-rock band Blivet Eye and an exponent of feminist theology.

In the early years of this century a most unseemly controversy arose. Otto Scheidt, a Bavarian who had acquired British citizenship as a result of a clerical error at the Home Office, had already achieved some notoriety when he stood as a parliamentary candidate for Brobmore Regis and was bound over to keep the peace following numerous complaints about his canvassing techniques, which included playing a tuba outside prospective voters' homes at six a.m. Alleging that his grandmother had been the illegitimate daughter of Spencer Gibbon, he lodged a claim against Lady Ariel in the county court for possession of the golden arm, which he insisted belonged rightfully to him. Although Spencer Gibbon is known to have taken several holidays in Bavaria in the 1870s, there was scant evidence to support Scheidt's claim and the case was dismissed. However, this did not stop him pursuing his claim with numerous appeals and letters to the press until he was arrested for entering a highly venomous jellyfish in the Crachelton-on-Sea Jellyfish Races with the intention of incapacitating the Swallows Brewery team.

By and large Stiltshire folk tend not to be avid sports fans but football and cricket are practised (rugby has never caught on, probably because most men fail to see the attraction of falling over on frozen ground or thrusting one's head into a seething mass of sweaty buttocks) along with some more unusual pastimes.

Sir Gideon Lancer (1803-78) was a spin-bowler and founder of Stiltshire County Cricket Club in 1856. Something of a folk hero, he made no money from his sporting prowess and steadfastly refused to give up his job as a sievewright.

Tommy Volesworth (1920-98) was Stiltshire's most famous footballer. He played 1,109 league games for Stiltford Elbow between 1939 and 1970 and scored a record 17 goals against Pawtley Mugs on 13th November 1954 (score 18-1).

Jack Jar (1927-2005), goalkeeper for the "Gravediggers" (Everbone FC) from 1946-64, is said to be the only goalie who was a match for Tommy Volesworth.

In the Stiltshire League both players and fans are intensely loyal to their local team. Games also attract admirers from further afield, like the couple from Liverpool who said "We love coming to Stiltshire for the footie; you get more goals for your money. And the pork pies are better!"

There is a racecourse at Twixham Market and the Marquess of Eyvesborough Stakes in July has traditionally provided an opportunity for dressing up and indulging in Pimm's and cream teas, but the bookmakers' takings are modest; Stiltshiremen, unless they come from Lonchelsea, are not much inclined to betting.

The art of bell ringing is enormously popular in Stiltshire. Almost all the bells in the county are ringable (the few exceptions being due to serious structural problems) and towers seldom struggle to find recruits. When the Stilchester Diocesan Guild of Church Bell Ringers (founded in 1831 by the Rev'd Edwin Puddle) holds its annual striking competition, huge crowds of both ringers and non-ringers turn out to listen and nearby pubs need to triple their normal weekly quota of ale.

A more esoteric event is the Pig and Toboggan Race which takes place on Ryming Head in the New Year, if and when there is sufficient snow on the North Drones. Teams of two are equipped with a pig (within strict weight limits) and a device which is a cross between a toboggan and a wheelbarrow. The pig has to be wheeled from the starting post up to the top of the hill, where the wheels are hastily removed from the toboggan and the team, including the pig, slides down a steep meandering slope to the finishing line. Each team may have up to three attempts, with their best time counting, but most understandably settle for one.

[See also the Christmas Pudding Olympics.]

The Jellyfish Races

The annual Jellyfish Races have been held at Crachelton-on-Sea every Summer since Victorian times. Two trenches, 200 feet long by 4 feet wide and 3 foot 6 deep, are dug in the firm sand and filled with sea water. There are two events: The Assisted Race is a knock-out competition for teams of four humans plus one jellyfish, the former having to propel the latter without touching it from one end of the trench to the other. There is often an exciting finish, tensions run high and accusations of touching, which if substantiated lead to disqualification, are common.

The Unassisted Race is altogether different. Several competing jellyfish are placed in one trench and have to make their own way to the finishing line. This can take some time, particularly on a windless day, and the water may need topping up more than once. The slowest time on record was 37h 46m in 1972.

Tragedy struck in 2000 when Miss Crachelton-on-Sea, Melissa Gammon (22), was mortally stung by a Portuguese man o' war. The creature, named Hernandes, was entered in the Unassisted Race by the UoS Department of Marine Biology. On being released from its tank, Hernandes flailed its way down the course with astonishing speed, leaving the other competitors drifting aimlessly in his wake, to cross the finishing line in an unprecedented 12m 43s, faster than some competitors in the Assisted Race.

Miss Gammon, who was there to present the trophies and clad only in a pink Helena Cressett bikini and her "Miss Crachleton-on-Sea" sash, murmured "Isn't he a sweetie?", whereupon she jumped into the water and attempted to hug the jellyfish. Seconds later, screaming in agony, she was dragged from the trench by horrified stewards. Paramedics were at the scene within minutes but by this time Miss Gammon, most of her body red and swollen, had begun to suffer respiratory failure. She died that evening in Crachelton Cottage Hospital. The Coroner's inquest returned a verdict of accidental death.

Under the rules of the Crachelton races, highly venomous species are barred from the Assisted Race for obvious reasons, but have always been permitted in the Unassisted event, though seldom used. Melissa's distraught parents, Bob and Marilyn Gammon, declined to take action against the race organisers or the UoS Department of Marine Biology. Said Bob "She always was an impulsive lass and never very hot on biology."

A Couturier and Patron of the Arts

Helena Cressett was born at Merribourne near Apstrow in 1860 and grew up in a staunchly Roman Catholic family. St Jude's in Apstrow is easily the most ostentatiously decorated church in the county. It possesses an unrivalled collection of exotic vestments and a monstrous monstrance which both fascinated and terrified the young Helena on its weekly appearance at Benediction. She later acknowledged that it was these aspects of her Catholic upbringing which fired her artistic imagination and inspired her work in the fashion industry.

In 1887 she opened a small boutique in Apstrow to sell her own designs which soon became a firm favourite with society ladies including the Marchioness of Eyvesborough. Success prompted a move to larger premises where she employed a growing army of seamstresses. Young girls dreamed of joining her team of sophisticated salesgirls, cosmeticists and models. Later in her career she encouraged and promoted a new generation of designers like Giovanna Giacometti with her classic Italian style and Emerald Ascot whose thoroughly modern outfits were a big hit in the 1920s.

Helena Cressett was a generous patron of the arts and ploughed most of her fortune into the eponymous galleries on the riverside in Apstrow. She died in 1934, having accidentally poisoned herself when she mistook a sample of a new perfume for a gin and French.

Brogue's Department Store

Standing opposite Helena Cressett's Fashion House in St Benedict Street is the largest retail outlet in Stiltshire, whose founder, coincidentally, was born in the house next door to Miss Cressett, albeit some years later.

Colonel George Haven Brogue (1895 – 1988) spent most of his military career in India where he met and married the daughter of a Maharajah, acquiring a substantial fortune in the process. On his return to England he set about converting a row of rather grand Georgian houses into the mighty emporium which we see today. Overhanging the street is a massive clock, the work of the Shrokeby horologist Harold Ploggs, which strikes the hours and quarters most melodiously on a chime of 17 bells hidden in the roof.

Brogue's Department Store, where one can buy almost anything from a last-minute wedding present to an obscure blend of China tea, a Tibetan singing bowl or a Hungarian goose down duvet and where ladies lunch after having their hair done, is still in the hands of the family, ably managed by George's grandson Martin. Two other well-known members of the dynasty are the former Tory MP William Brogue and his brother Hilary Brogue QC.

Art, Nihilism and Pyrotechnics

Artists do not feature prominently in the early history of Stiltshire, the only work of note being the anonymous mediaeval fresco *The Nativity* in St Mildred's church, Prumeford, better known as *The Adoration of the Porci* as it features a family of pigs in place of the customary ox and ass. In the late-Victorian era some local watercolourists achieved mild acclaim, including Charlotte Pike whose still life depictions of musical instruments with fruit were much sought-after.

Immanuel Lentil

Probably the county's most famous artist, Immanual Lentil (1899 - 1954) was born in Stilhaven, the son of a Romanian sailor and a local barmaid. He was subsequently adopted by the Harbourmaster Joshua Lentil and his wife Fanny and brought up in comfortable if austere surroundings. A lonely and introverted child, he was prone to quirky displays of emotion, such as embracing statues for whom he felt sorry at their being left out in the rain. His artistic talents became apparent at a tender age and his infantile pictures of stick figures with featureless faces were a precursor of the mood of negativity which was to characterise his early period.

While he was still an undergraduate at Stangley Hall, Lentil's work began to attract critical acclaim and many of his unusual still life paintings were exhibited at the Stilhaven Gallery during the 1920's. During this time he began a tempestuous affair with a fellow student, Lady Amanda Snebwood, widely believed to be the model for his "nude" series. When she eventually married a greengrocer from Shrokeby, the grief-stricken artist expressed his despair by drinking large quantities of Aqua Discorpus and painting self-portraits in which coffins, embalming fluid and other funerary paraphernalia featured prominently. An attempt to drown himself in Stilhaven harbour was narrowly thwarted by a salvage crew failing to recover the remnants of the Stiltmouth Floating Railway who inadvertently brought his near-lifeless body to the surface.

Invited to contribute to the Royal Academy Summer Exhibition in 1932, Lentil responded by severing his right thumb and forefinger with a breadknife and submitting the three items in a collage enigmatically titled *The Means Justifieth the End*. After this, his work took a marked change of direction, the bold, firm brush strokes of his earlier canvases giving way to a more tentative, fragmented style. His subject matter was different too, showing a preoccupation with obscure religious themes such as *Solomon and his Concubine Listening to the Voice of the Turtle* (1936). Despite widespread acknowledgment of his artistic genius, he became increasingly reclusive, rarely being seen in public apart from an annual appearance in the Gruntlington Carnival dressed as a giraffe.

Lentil's output in his final years was sparse and ever more esoteric. *The Spectre of Flatulence*, though one of his best-known works, defies rational explanation or even informed analysis. In 1953 he took up residence in a flimsy wooden hut on St Magg's Island, where he died of pneumonia the following winter. Some authorities argue that *Anti-dawn of Being*, completed days before his death, represents the culmination of a lifelong devotion to nihilism; others believe it to be a final tribute to his adoptive aunt Dawn Fishwife, Lentil having once remarked that his childhood memories of her broad-bosomed embrace were his only refuge from a hostile universe.

A permanent exhibition of his works opened at the Helena Cressett Galleries in Apstrow in 1999. Among the seminal works featured are:
Still Life Without Pomegranates (1926)
Featureless Landscape (1927)
Nude with Clothes On (1927)
Portrait of an Headless Man (1928)
Still Life Without Bowls, Fruit, Flowers, Bottles and Tablecloth (1928)
Sleeping Nude with Woollen Pajamas (1929)
Still Life Without Inanimate Objects (1929)
The Earth Without Form and Void (1933)
The Capitulation of St Anthony (1941)
The Penultimate Supper (1942)
Job Lancing his Boils (1942)
St Francis Feeding the Slugs (1943)
The Spectre of Flatulence (1949)
The Twilight of Continence (1951)
Anti-dawn of Being (1953)

Wayne Larder

A contemporary artist who admits to being inspired by Lentil's work, Wayne Larder has a penchant for working with offal and explosives. Typical of his oeuvre is *My Bath* (2001), a small room featuring a scum-lined bathtub and a pile of soiled towels and crumpled underpants; at certain times of day (entirely at the whim of the artist), a pair of kidneys may be seen in the wash basin. Exhibitions of his work are frequently accompanied by culinary pyrotechnics such as exploding faggots or rockets trailing strings of incandescent sausages.

His most famous creation *Homage to Horace*, first realised in 1998 and consisting of five giant Catherine wheels made from sheep's entrails stuffed with gunpowder, earned him a degree of notoriety in 2002 when it malfunctioned and set fire to the west wing of the Helena Cressett Galleries, causing £5,000,000 worth of damage. Although several of his other pieces were destroyed in the blaze, Mr Larder came to regard the incident as the highlight of his career.

The Exception

If you have read thus far, you have no doubt realised what a delightful place Stiltshire is. Perhaps you are even beginning to wish you lived there. But regrettably I have to tell you, dear reader, that there is one corner of this idyllic county which is not like the rest of it – the seaside town of Lonchelsea.

As seaside towns go, it has neither the genteel splendour of Brobmore Regis with its Regency buildings, ornamental chine and maroon and gold vintage trams, nor the neo-Edwardian kitsch of Crachelton-on-Sea with its elegant pier, Punch and Judy show, ice cream parlours, whelk stalls and rock shops.

Lonchelsea is full of caravan sites, tacky amusement arcades, bingo halls, betting shops and fast-food outlets selling execrable burgers or pizzas that would make an Italian want to throw up. People drink cheap, nasty lager (not of course produced by any Stiltshire brewery) and wear baseball caps, shell suits and chunky, tasteless gold jewellery. The churches are almost empty. Police statistics reveal that 94% of all crimes* dealt with by the Stiltshire Constabulary are committed in Lonchelsea. Indeed, the whole ethos of the place is the antithesis of the character and values which make Stiltshire what it is.

You may wonder how this sorry state of affairs came about. It was not ever thus; at one time Lonchelsea was much like any other town. The pubs sold decent ale, the churches were full and the nearest thing to fast food came from three seafront fish and chip shops. But gradually, over the early to middle decades of the 20th century, it became as it is now. Sociologists have attributed the change to a phenomenon called "sociopathic coagulation": given increased social mobility, the undesirable types tend to gravitate to a common environment. But why Lonchelsea? No-one knows. The best explanation anyone has come up with is that it's all to do with the name - it simply isn't euphonious.

But it may well be that Lonchelsea's downfall was foretold by a 12th century mystic, St Gillian of Flover. As a teenager she began to experience visions, including a recurring one where the Archangel Raphael wielded a great sieve in which human souls were sifted and purified. For the rest of her life she alternated between periods of devotion, contemplation and composing music at Flover Priory and touring the countryside exhorting the peasantry to piety, chastity and charity. She was not an ascetic however and well known for her enjoyment of good food and ale. In her final vision, Raphael declared that "the heathen will thrive in the Land of Lunca". The church of St Gillian, Brobhampton, stands closed to the supposed site of her birth which is now the Brobmore Regis tram depot. St Gillian has been adopted as the patron saint of sievewrights and tram drivers.

* The remaining 6% is largely accounted for by Oxbake and Jupton.

Speaking of Stiltshire

Dialects

The native tongue of Stiltshire is a gentle, faintly rustic accent which varies slightly across the county from east to west. Vowels tend to be a little longer in the fishing villages of Dongland and the cider-making Chineham area than on the moors of the north-east. Hazedale has its own peculiar dialect, still spoken in the villages of Hazzock and Goadinger [See the Christmas carol The Goadinger Clarion].

Stiltshire folk (except those from Lonchelsea) tend to grow up with a love of words and greatly admire a rich and poetic turn of phrase. To outsiders the grammar and vocabulary can sound old-fashioned, even archaic. Usage of the second person singular persisted long after it had died out in most parts of England. Indeed, even today many people still use the words thee and thou when addressing their nearest and dearest and, of course, the Almighty. Modern forms of liturgy have found little favour in the pews of the Diocese of Stilchester.

The Motto of Stiltshire

Dominus subulcus meus est

"The Lord is my swineherd"

Stiltshire Proverbs and Expressions

to give (something) the blivet eye

> to examine critically (from the work of the cheese conner)

(to be) a Pawtley Mugg

> silly or clumsy (an expression used occasionally in east Stiltshire, much to the annoyance of players and supporters of Pawtley FC)

as hard as Tommy Thickness' sausage

> a reference to the dense sausages produced in the village of Thickness.

piglet

> a common term of endearment

as fit as Snebwood's horse

> ready for the knacker's yard (a reference to Sir Roderick Snebwood who was notoriously hard on his horses)

sorry as Bezzle or *(to make) Bezzle's repentance*

> not sorry at all (a reference to the felon and blasphemer Jacob Bezzle who refused to repent even on the gallows)

You don't need a hogshead to pickle a hog's head.

> Don't go over the top (a play on words, commonly used to urge restraint).

A sieve is holier than a chalice.

> You can't always judge by appearances (another play on words).

Red sky, shepherd's pie.

> There are more important topics of conversation than the weather (e.g. where one's next meal is coming from).

Watercress winsome, parsnip plump.

> You are what you eat (a reference to pig feeding practices).

You don't get good crackling from a lean pig.

> Shallow people don't make good company.

No use staring at the sunset.

> What's done is done (a reference to Bishop Odfranc).

Stiltshire Nursery Rhymes

'Twas on a January day
The North wind blew the pigs away.
They floated over wood and hill,
O'er castle grand and lowly mill,
Until they came to rest, good people,
On the top of Shrokeby steeple.

[Nursery rhyme common in East Stiltshire.]

~~~~~~~~~~~~~

Jupton people feed on slugs,
Jupton people smell,
Jupton people harbour bugs
And widdle in the well.

[Traditional children's rhyme from Oxbake.]

~~~~~~~~~~~~~

Corncrake, corncrake, fly to Oxbake.
Make a noise to wake the dead.
Rouse the parson out of bed.
Drop a blessing on his head.

[A rather mild version of a popular Jupton ditty.]

~~~~~~~~~~~~~

Here we go Jiggery Jearing across the fields so green.
We all go Jiggery Jearing to choose the Summer Queen
With garlands gay and frittles of hay while onions keep the devil away,
We'll crown a big fat nanny goat, the fairest ever seen.

[The twin villages of Jearing All Saints and Jearing St Thomas have a long history of goat-rearing. This song is sung by children at an annual festival in July when a nanny goat is crowned as the Summer Queen. A frittle is a local and rather ornate form of hay bale upon which the judges in this caprine beauty contest sit. Onions are traditionally fed to the contestants to ensure they remain free from demonic possession.]

One Mong, two Mong, three Mong, four,
Five Mong, six Mong, seven,
Eight Mong, Greyt Mong, you're the one I hate, Mong,
You're the one who'll never get to Heaven.
Plappp!!!

One Mong, two Mong, ...

[Dipping chant from Dongland. On the word "Plappp", the child last pointed to by the dipper is unceremoniously pushed out of the circle and counting begins again until only one participant is left.]

~~~~~~~~~~~~~~

Fee-futty-fie-bo,
Old man come, baby go.

[One of the strangest characters in Stiltshire folklore, Fee-futty-fie-bo is said to appear in alternate years as a tiny wizened old man or a gigantic baby. In the former guise he is believed to be relatively harmless but in the latter form may carry off and eat piglets or naughty children.]

~~~~~~~~~~~~~~

Grumblin' Grandpa Gribley's Ghost
Eats fried boys on buttered toast.
Silly, heedless little chaps,
He will catch them in his traps.
Phatty Philip, Dithering Dan,
See them sizzling in the pan.
Slothful Stephen, Nutty Ned,
Salt and peppered, laid on bread.
Lazy Lionel, Kareless Keith,
He will gnash them with his teeth,
Spit the bones out on the floor,
Keep the fat to oil the door.

[Girls' skipping rhyme of comparatively modern origin. Arthur Hubert Gribley (d. 1930) was an extraordinarily cantankerous old man who lived in Smitley and seemed to spend much of his time threatening children with various gardening implements.]

Some Literary Persons of Note

Jeromey Flanhead

An eccentric even by Stiltshire standards, Jeromey Flanhead (1836-1900) was a Fellow of Stangley Hall who achieved a measure of notoriety through the publication of a number of outrageous religious tracts. He was particularly interested in the testimony of Balham de Pailey, the mad 9th Duke of Stiltshire, concerning his extra-terrestrial mentor, Morfark, and made a detailed study of the Duke's papers written during his imprisonment on Gryatt Island. It was he who popularised the idea that the three wise men were in fact Morfark and his companions Prennix and Eeybalborp and the star of Bethlehem their spaceship.

Flanhead was known to be addicted to the monastic beverage Aqua Discorpus and at one stage kidnapped a member of each of the three families who produced it in an attempt to make them reveal the original recipe.

Nicodemus Mayce

A near-contemporary of Flanhead but of an altogether more sober disposition, Nicodemus Mayce (1817-1900) was known as a philosopher, philanthropist and politician (he was Liberal MP for Brobmore Regis from 1842-75). His epic poem "Pity the Simpleton" has inspired generations of writers and musicians.

Sidney Antrobus Pillion

Born in Apstrow in 1840 and educated at Stangley Hall, where he read literature and history, Pillion began writing for the Stiltshire Gazette in his mid-twenties and quickly achieved recognition for his acerbic comments on the great and good of the day. He wrote a few satirical plays but is chiefly remembered for his collaboration with the composer George Crumbleforth, writing the lyrics to 19 comic operettas.

His personal life might reasonably be described as less than successful; none of his nine marriages lasted more than a few months, most of his wives declaring him arrogant, spiteful and impossible to live with. His only son, from his fourth marriage to Candice Lunch, entered a monastery at the age of 17 and never spoke to his father again.

The partnership with Crumbleforth ended acrimoniously in 1900 and the announcement, two years later, of the composer's knighthood provoked a series of extremely vitriolic (even by his standards) letters to his former collaborator, the King, the Prime Minister and the national and local press. Thereafter he withdrew from public life and died, a lonely and embittered man, in 1911.

Oliver Mayce

A short balding man with a goatee beard and a tremulous tenor voice, Oliver

Mayce (1841-1908) was Professor of Mathematics at St Cedd's. He is chiefly remembered, however, for his encyclopaedia of cheese, "A Word about Curd". His first wife Marguerite Mayce (no relation) was the daughter of Nicodemus (qv).

Amethyst von Houghton

Amethyst (1866-1926), daughter of the Rector of Lydegar Decorum, began writing at the age of 16. Her early novels have been criticised in some quarters as being boring - the heroines are always pretty but chaste, the heroes gentlemanly to the point of nausea, and they always live happily ever after - but she had a way with words; there are some extremely subtle plot twists and delightful depictions of the Stiltshire countryside.

Her mature works scandalised Edwardian society (Gruntlington Band of Hope tried unsuccessfully to have "Lord Rodney's Maid" banned) but became enormously popular with the Flappers in the 1920s. She was the wife of Rear-Admiral Malachi Medlar and the mother of Alfred Medlar (qv).

Lady Annabelle de Pailey

The younger daughter of Sir Arthur Dimley-Potts of Pattershawm Grange, Annabelle (1866-1954) grew up to be an elegant and cultured young lady. In 1890 she married Clive de Pailey, a dashing young officer shortly to become the 16th Marquess of Eyvesborough, in what was described as the Stiltshire wedding of the decade. Sadly the Marquess died in the Great War, run down by an armoured vehicle.

As Dowager Marchioness of Eyvesborough, Lady Annabelle became widely respected for her charitable works and much in demand as an opener of fêtes. She began writing shortly after her husband's death and produced a number of improving children's books including: "How Peter the Pony became Archbishop of Gallopbury", "Digby Mole MP defeats those frightful Socialists" and her best-seller "Sidney the Kidney" (a child's introduction to anatomy).

Alan Bletwood

The poet, toper and otherwise good-for-nothing Alan Bletwood (1874-1937) was born, lived and died in Oxbake. He never had a proper job but made sufficient money for his beer and food by reciting poetry of his own composition (often made up on the spot) in the village's pubs. He also wrote the song "Oxbake Ale", supposedly inspired by the sound of the bells of Oxbake church. After he died such fragments of his work as he had written down or could be remembered by his drinking companions were compiled into a slim anthology and published by Oxbake Brewery.

Alfred Medlar

The son of Rear-Admiral Malachi Medlar and the novelist Amethyst von Houghton (qv), Alfred (1896-1968) was regarded as being shy and socially inept and had a very distant relationship with his father. He studied theology at Stangley Hall and was ordained in 1919. He served two curacies, at Jupton and Kings Pebberworth, before resigning from the ministry on the kindly advice of the Rev'd Ezra Rhodes of Thrimp, who discerned that the young man's evident tendencies might be a serious obstacle to future preferment.

Alfred then discovered in himself a talent for writing gruesome horror stories and published his first book "Kill me slowly" in 1930. Around this time he set up home with his life-long companion, the playwright Guy Thame (qv), in a fisherman's cottage near St Togan where they lived for many years and were known to their neighbours as "those nice young men".

Guy Thame

Guy Thame (1901-1970), born in Fudwell, had an unhappy childhood. His father died when he was three and his mother three years later, leaving him the ward of his uncle Timothy Tobias (TT) Waddington, the unscrupulous and much-loathed Chief Executive of the Stilchester Central Bank. After being cared for by a succession of nannies, he went to the Stilchester Academy as a boarder and then to St Cedd's, where he was still unhappy but revealed a talent for writing which was encouraged by the Professor of Literature, Irwin Pencil.

After modest success with a few short playlets, he achieved fame in 1928 when his semi-autobiographical play "The Irrelevance of being Luke Warm" was put on at the Elysium theatre, Apstrow, with the celebrated actor Sebastian Thrice-Wessley in the title role. This was followed (1932) by a satirical work "The Banker" based on the life of his (now dead) uncle.

Jocasta Spreadeagle

Jocasta (1923-2004) was born in Obervole and in her childhood was an avid reader, particularly enjoying the romantic novels of Amethyst von Houghton (qv). Her own style, however, proved to be even more racy. Her first novel "Swineherds' Kisses", published in 1946 is a steamy rustic romp and was followed by several more in the same genre. In 1957 she came under harsh criticism from the Bishop of Stilchester for her portrayal of the clergy in "Dog Collar" (said to have been inspired by the ghost of the naked curate at the Three Tuns in Obervole, who allegedly died wearing nothing but his clerical collar). "The Putrid Heart" (1970) marked a change of direction where love and lust were intertwined with an intriguing murder mystery. In all, she wrote 36 novels.

A Taste of Stiltshire

Pork

Pork features prominently in the Stiltshire diet. The county has its own distinctive breeds of pig: the Prumeford Russet, Smoatham Saddleback, Pride of Aggerby and the now rare Rimpleham.

Prumeford Pig Pie

For this recipe, pigs' trotters are simmered to produce a thick, unctuous gravy in which chunks of pork (usually belly) and pig's kidney are cooked with onions and wild herbs and covered with a crumbly short-crust pastry. Purists insist that the trotters should be left in the pie and gnawed after the rest has been eaten.

Thickness Sausage

The little village of Thickness on the coast produces a unique type of pork sausage, heavy and dense of texture with an intense meaty flavour, robustly spiced. A cold Thickness sausage dropped onto an enamel plate from a height of a foot or more should produce a resounding clang.

Strupton Sausages

These are small, reddish in colour and almost spherical. Whilst they may be cooked in a rich sauce and served with mashed potato or pasta, they are often eaten cold and frequently sold in pubs as a bar snack.

Brawn

No part of the pig is wasted, and the head is usually used to make brawn, which is often eaten at tea-time on thick chunks of granary bread with a dollop of mustard and a sprig of watercress. Biddy Bullock (1864-1962), a celebrated brawn maker from Martyr Pebberworth is immortalised in song.

Cheeses

Chineham

A hard cheese with a rich, nutty flavour. First mentioned in the annals of St Cedd's College over 500 years ago, it is still made at a handful of farms around Chineham Gregory and Little Chineham. Resisting any attempts at modernisation, these family businesses continue to make the cheese in large truckles and normally mature it for at least a year. A good wedge of Chineham with a hunk of granary bread and fresh butter and a little pickled crab apple makes a sound lunch, especially when accompanied by a quart of the local cider which complements it admirably.

Repstock

A pale, crumbly cheese with a slightly acidic flavour. Repstock has been made for centuries on the slopes of the North Drones. Commercial production has all too often turned a mild cheese into a bland one and Repstock has unfortunately suffered from this trend since the 1950s. Farmhouse Repstock is rare, though slowly making a come-back, but possesses a subtlety which makes it well worth seeking out. It is often eaten at Advent with a slice of fruit cake and a glass of Madeira wine.

Blefton Blue

A firm but creamy cheese with extensive blue veining. It is only made at Blefton and matured in the caverns of Blefton Burrows, where the ambient temperature is ideal for the purpose. Connoisseurs claim to be able to tell by the degree of saltiness whether a particular cheese was stored at the landward or the seaward end of the cave system. Blefton is a perfect after dinner cheese, served with slivers of ripe pear and a glass of port.

Blivet

Blivet (or blivit) represents a style of cheesemaking peculiar to Stiltshire: a soft, pungent cheese made from pigs' milk. Until the latter part of the 19th century it was made all over the swine-rearing area between Aggerby and Scrunton and eaten regularly by the peasantry. Then tastes changed, production declined and by the 1960s Blivet was all but extinct. However, during recent years several young cheesemakers have revived the craft and Blivet, though definitely an acquired taste, has achieved something of a cult following. Indeed, the Hogberrow Michaelmas Fair and Blivit Market has once more become an annual event after a lapse of some 240 years.

As yet, the post of Cheese Conner has not been resurrected, but in mediaeval times these arbiters of quality were, like their colleagues the Ale Conners, highly respected members of the community. The phrase "to give it the blivet eye" originates from the work of the Cheese Conner and means to examine something critically.

Brewing

There are three substantial breweries still working in Stiltshire - Oxbake Brewery Company, Swallows of Eyvesborough and Aliment's Anchor Ales in Stilhaven. In the past, of course, there were many more. In recent years several new small breweries have opened, following the success of the Knorrley Forest microbrewery.

Swallow & Nephew's Brewery

Tinker's Row, Eyvesborough

Prudence Swallow (b. 1745) was an Eyvesborough ale wife who ran a tavern in Stork Street. A stocky, ruddy-faced woman, she was much respected by her customers for the wholesomeness of her ale and the orderliness of her house. Although short in stature, she would have no hesitation in throwing a burly navvy over the threshold when he had taken a drop too much. If her physical presence was daunting, her verbal dominance of all she encountered was legendary; the tongue of Prudence could bend the ear of any man, high or lowly, into abject submission within minutes. And when she took it into her head to extend her trade, many were the lobes that bit the dust: town councillors, Members of Parliament, leaders of the nascent temperance movement and anyone else who stood in the way of her ambitions. When she died in 1831, her grandson inherited a brewery producing 5,000 barrels a week and 43 tied houses. She is commemorated in one of the twelve statues of local worthies erected by the Victorian builders of the splendid neo-gothic Town Hall.

Her great-great-granddaughter, also called Prudence, much resembled her illustrious ancestor both in temperament and appearance. On becoming Mrs Herbert Loampit in 1903, she chose to retain her maiden name for the sake of the family identity, and was known as an extremely shrewd businesswoman who, between 1912 and 1942, expanded the company to the extent that today Swallow's brewery has a near monopoly of the licensed trade in east Stiltshire, having taken over Spraints of Ryming (1930), Jorrocks of Jupton (1938) and Groats of Church Plean (1955) as well as several smaller establishments. The current proprietors are Sir Dudley and Lady Ariel Swallow.

Oxbake Brewery Company

Oaks Yard, Oxbake

There has been a brewery on this site for at least 400 years. Oxbake ales are highly regarded (except by Jupton folk) and praised for their miraculous properties in the well-known song "Oxbake Ale".

Early in the 20th century the Oxbake brewery came under the control of Joseph Strenshaw, a younger son of an established Stilchester brewing family. He immediately embarked upon an ambitious expansion programme, taking over the other two Stilchester brewers, Trant (in 1906) and Archangel (1913) as well as the Prokeworth brewery (1911), home of the famous Prokeworth Porter, still brewed by Oxbake today.

Eventually, in 1924, he bought out his own brother Edwin, closed the Chaddlestead Road premises in Stilchester and dropped the Strenshaw name, thus ending 214 years of brewing history and sparking a family feud which smoulders to this day.

With the acquisition of Dew's of Debble (1955) and Undergates of Tworpsbridge (1962), OBC expanded its trading area into Dongland and now, apart from the resurgence of Aliment's in the Stilhaven area, enjoys a dominance of the licensed trade in west Stiltshire comparable to that of Swallow's in the east.

Aliment and Sons

Anchorage Brewery, Eastbutts, Stilhaven

Founded by Thomas Aliment in 1786, this brewery once served over 50 pubs in Stilhaven and the surrounding villages. 'Twas often said that Aliments's Anchor Ales stopped the sailors roaming and for this reason were unpopular with certain businesswomen in the town. Sadly, the brewery was forced to close in 1966.

However, 18 years later, young Jason Aliment, grandson of the last proprietor and an enthusiast for traditional ales, opened a microbrewery in the old premises. Such was the success of his beers made to ancestral recipes that he was gradually able to renovate most of the old equipment and bring it back into use. In 1990 the opportunity arose to buy back a dozen of Aliment's former pubs from Oxbake Brewery Co. and now the output of the brewery is rapidly approaching its former capacity.

Knorrley Forest Brewery

Abraham's Shed, Branladen Lane, Shuckerton, Obervole

Established in 1995, when Adam Crackling and Tim Door, two former accountants who became terminally bored with city life and decided to do something worthwhile, set up this tiny microbrewery in a converted barn near Obervole.

The beers have proved popular in the free trade, and they are looking to purchase their first tied house. Their infamous Henbane Ale was taken off the market after a short trial period in 1997 after drinkers complained about the life-threatening side-effects.

The Porcine Pub Company   30 Church Yew Street, Hogberrow

Stiltshire's only non-brewing pub chain. The ambitious company was the brainchild of entrepreneur Simon Toast, who first opened the Saddleback Inn in the disused Hogberrow post office in 1989. The company has been converting redundant premises into pubs across the county since then and now has nine houses in total, including Stiltshire's largest pub, the Gammon Ham in Gruntlington (a former printing works). The pubs are all decorated in a "piggy" theme, and all of them sell Swallow's EPA and Oxbake Mild * plus a range of guest beers and are renowned for their home-made pork scratchings.

* apart from The Sow in Jupton which sells Swallow's Prudence Mild instead.

Cider Making

Farms in the Chineham area still make traditional "honest" cider (pure apple juice fermented with wild yeast, nothing added and nothing taken away) from their own orchards. Chineham cider is invariably dry, fruity and strong and is either sold young and cloudy or kept for two or three years when it clears naturally and mellows beautifully; this "venerable" cider as it is known is normally drunk on festivals or birthdays.

Cider making is in Chineham's blood and many households in the area have a small and antiquated cider press with which they make modest quantities for domestic consumption.

Aqua Discorpus

A powerful liqueur distilled from elderflower wine with a secret blend of herbs and floral extracts, Aqua Discorpus was originally made by the monks of Scrunton Abbey. The name allegedly refers to the "out of body experience" sometimes described by those who drink it to excess, although it is in all probability a corruption of "Aqua de Corvus", after the crows which have always frequented the grounds of Scrunton Abbey. Rumours that it contains macerated corvine entrails or the blood of a black sow spilt at the new moon - should be taken with a pinch of salt.

Received wisdom has it that, after the dissolution of the monasteries, one Brother Reginald vouchsafed the recipe to three local families: the Fulgoods of Scrunton, the Obsides of Flunt and the Trants of Eftmere, but each version was lacking one of the 37 ingredients. Clandestine production continued throughout the years of religious persecution and right up to the end of the Civil War, when large quantities of Aqua Discorpus were drunk publicly to celebrate the restoration of the monarchy. By this time, each of the three families having closely guarded its own recipe for over a century, they were unwilling to pool their knowledge and so the three versions continued to be made independently and the recipes handed down by word of mouth from one generation to the next.

By the mid-19th century, Aqua Discorpus was extremely fashionable among the county gentry and the academics of Stilchester. Obside, Trant and Fulgood each had its devotees and connoisseurs would argue endlessly over the respective merits of the three. Some would blend them in an attempt to recreate the "Scrunton Abbey Elixir" but it was noted that, whilst the blend should in theory contain all the ingredients of the original, three of them must necessarily be in reduced proportions. Pleas for co-operation between the makers fell upon deaf ears. One fanatic, Jeromey Flanhead, even kidnapped a member of each family and threatened them with torture, but all declared they would rather die than yield their secrets and they were soon rescued by a band of addicts who feared that all three recipes might be lost.

Then, in 1883, Samuel Obside died suddenly without passing on "the knowledge". For a while it seemed that all hope of reconstructing Brother Reginald's recipe was lost for ever until the mathematician Augustus Steed (he of "Inn Sign" fame) pointed out that, assuming it was true that each recipe lacked one ingredient (as opposed to having a unique extra ingredient), all the ingredients must still be present in the Fulgood and/or Trant versions. Renewed pressure was put upon those families. It was at this stage that some people began to invoke a previously unheard-of prophecy to the effect that the ruins of Scrunton Abbey would crumble into dust if the true Aqua Discorpus were ever to be brewed again.

The happy ending to this story came about quite by chance. In 1962, two Stilchester dons, Dr Michael Blosworth from Old College and Professor Alfred Stroble from St Cedd's, were lunching together in the Bishop and Sunset. Each had recently been examining manuscripts from Scrunton Abbey in his own college archives and it transpired that each had found a scrap of paper with a list of simples written thereon. When the two lists were compared, they were obviously written in the same hand, as were other documents identifying the writer as Brother Cecil and one referring to "my esteemed assistant, Brother Reginald". It dawned upon the pair that they were looking at nothing less than two halves of the original recipe for Aqua Discorpus.

A meeting was convened at which the heads of the Fulgood and Trant clans, after some initial reluctance to take part, confirmed the discovery and were rewarded with the revelation of each other's extra ingredient. The Fulgoods were aware of every item on Brother Cecil's list except horehound, while the Trants used horehound but not purslane. Soon afterwards the two dons, both by happy coincidence from the village of Flunt, applied for and were granted a licence to distil the beverage. There were a few anxious glances cast at the walls of the Abbey as the first drops emerged from the still, but that venerable structure remains in no worse a state of disintegration than it has been for centuries.

Nowadays, Flunt Aqua Discorpus is sold alongside those of Fulgood and Trant, who both market an "Original" and a "Traditional" or "Family" version. Only one question remains unanswered: "What was the Obsides' missing ingredient?". Regrettably, there is no way of telling.

Bar Snacks

Jacob Comet's Cheesey Morsels

Jacob Oedipus Comet (1881-1965) was an Eyvesborough baker of some renown. In the 1930s he perfected what many have called the ultimate cheese biscuit with a strong flavour and just the right consistency between firm, crumbly and moist. Originally sold only in waxed paper bags from his shop, they became available to a wider clientele in the 1960s when his son Joseph found a way of sealing them into a cellophane bag without compromising the flavour or texture.

Although widely available in Stiltshire pubs, Jacob Comet's Cheesey Morsels differ from lesser cheese biscuits due to the exacting standards maintained by Jacob's great-grandson Richard. To this day, the best-before date is set a mere ten days after the packing date to ensure that they are enjoyed in a condition that the founder would be proud of.

While Jacob only ever used Chineham cheese, Repstock and Blefton Blue varieties have been available since the 1990s, although they account for less than 15% of sales. A brief experiment with Blivet flavoured Cheesey Morsels was not considered a success.

Stanley Carnage's Bacon Scones

Corporal Stanley Carnage (1912-99) was a cook in the Royal Stiltshire Regiment. One day in 1943, while stationed at Cauldby Barracks, he took delivery of two sides of bacon which consisted of an inordinate amount, nay, an unbelievable amount of fat and a scant helping of lean meat. Undeterred, he rendered down the fat, mixed it with flour and baking soda and created a large batch of scones to which he added the finely diced meat. The scones were an instant hit with the men and were subsequently served to the Commander-in-Chief, General Sir Arthur Limestone, who pronounced them "a gastronomic tour-de-force" and promptly promoted Carnage to Sergeant for his ingenuity.

After the war Carnage, with the General's encouragement and financial backing, set up a small business in his home town of Narkington to manufacture the bacon scones commercially. The recipe was slightly modified, with some of the bacon fat replaced by butter, and the scones soon became a much sought-after accompaniment to a pint or two of ale or cider, as well as being enjoyed in the genteel tea rooms of Apstrow and Brobmore Regis. When Stanley's son Gerald took over the business in 1978 he had to move to larger premises in order to keep up with demand.

Today the business is astutely run by Gerald's daughter Georgina Stanley Carnage (known to her friends and employees as George or Stanley respectively). A recent advertising campaign featured the Stilchester bass Quainton Rhodes and his old English sheepdog Gesualdo, who regularly accompanies him to the pub and has come to expect a couple of Stanley Carnage's Bacon Scones with his bowl of ale.

The Stiltshire Diet and Character

It has often been said that the amiable and stoical nature of Stiltshire folk owes much to their diet and their love of good food and drink.

Poor Noah Stubble was 100 years old
And 80 years wed to a fiery-tongued scold.
When folk said "Noah, you must be a saint
To live with that dragon without complaint",
He'd draw on his pipe and softly declare
"If truth be told I can't abide 'er,
But a man can bear anything, foul or fair,
On good roast pork and a flagon o' cider."

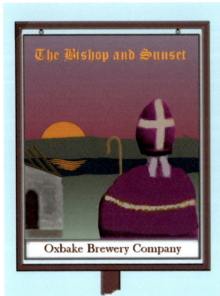

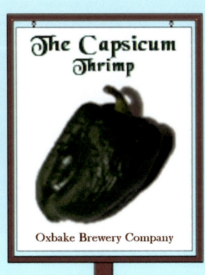

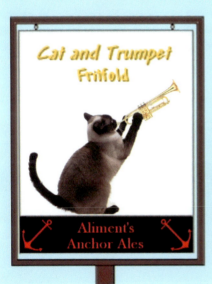

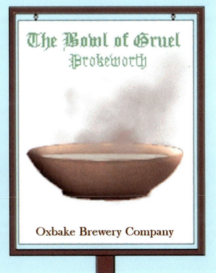

Like every English county, Stiltshire abounds with old - and not so old - inns: public houses they are in the best sense, homes-from-home, providing refreshment to the worker, shelter to the traveller, a refuge from domestic strife, a place wherein to set the world to rights. Their names are many and varied, and some of them have an interesting story to tell …

The Bishop and Sunset, Stilchester

This small but busy pub stands on the west bank of the Stilt, just outside the Cathedral precincts. There has been a house of refreshment on this site since time immemorial; the present building dates substantially from the sixteenth century and it is known to have been called the Bishop and Sunset since at least that time. The name recalls the disconsolate Bishop Odfranc gazing at the setting sun in the realisation that his plans had come to nought.

Beneath the bar is an enormous cellar, said to have been excavated by fourteenth century monks. Over the years it has satisfied the considerable thirsts of ringers, choristers, vergers and students and continues to do so as well as attracting a steady flow of tourists on account of its riverside setting and proximity to the Cathedral.

The Capsicum, Thrimp

This house owes its unusual name to the former Rector of Thrimp, the Rev'd Sidney Otter, and his habit of growing exotic vegetables in the Rectory, the vestry, under the altar and anywhere else where suitable conditions prevailed. The sign depicts a shrivelled green capsicum on one side and on the other the leaves and tendrils of the plant entwining the pulpit while the eccentric cleric intones a text from the book of Genesis, "And the earth brought forth grass and herb yielding seed after his kind, and the tree yielding fruit, whose seed was in itself, after his kind".

It is a small building, as befits a village of 70-odd souls, built in well-mellowed brick with a slate roof and covered with the foliage of assorted climbing plants, planted and nurtured by successive generations of licensees with regard to the horticultural traditions of the place. The bitter is often dry-hopped with flowers from the pub's own fuggles bine.

The Cat and Trumpet, Fritfold

Students of pub etymology will instantly recognise this name as being a corruption of "Catherine the Strumpet".

The lady in question was Catherine de Pailey, the youngest daughter of the eighth Marquess of Eyvesborough. In 1693 at the age of nineteen, in order to escape an arranged marriage to the tallow merchant Henry Chumpend, an extremely rich but loathsome personage with boils on his neck, she took the extreme action of riding to Stilhaven, boarding the nearest ship, the frigate *Imponderable*, and offering her favours to the entire crew. Standing upon the foredeck, she explained her mission and began divesting herself of her clothing, crying "He shall not wed a strumpet!".

At this point, the First Officer, a noble young fellow named Archer Medlar, seeing this comely redhead about to dispose of her virtue, abseiled down from the bridge, landing upon bended knee and straightway proposed to her. She, observing his muscular frame, kindly face and the lack of excrescences thereon, promptly accepted. The ratings, to their credit, averted their gaze while she resumed her raiment and then raised a lusty cheer to the newly betrothed couple. The Captain, on learning what all the noise was about, immediately commanded that the vessel put out into the harbour so that he might exercise his prerogative to marry them at sea.

Following a long and distinguished naval career, her husband became Admiral Sir Archer Medlar and was for many years High Sheriff of Stiltshire. Lady Medlar was renowned throughout the county for her charitable works and patronage of the arts but doomed forever to be known as Catherine the Strumpet, albeit more with affection than condemnation.

Quite when the name changed to its present form no-one knows although it may well have been during the Victorian era. Today the pub is an unpretentious, friendly local selling jolly good ale and, not inappropriately, a favourite haunt of jazz musicians.

The Bowl of Gruel, Prokeworth

This ancient inn has stood on the square at Prokeworth for centuries. It features in the ballad "Aiden o' Skent" and the tale of the headless butcher.

Often assumed by visitors to be of comparatively recent devising with Dickensian associations, the name Bowl of Gruel actually predates the local workhouse by at least two centuries. There are two possible explanations in local folklore.

The first takes the form of a legend. The Blessed Witta, passing through the town one winter's evening on his return from the shrine of St Botolph on Gryatt Island, stopped at a hovel and asked the good lady therein to spare him a morsel of food. The poor woman, having just fed the last crusts of a stale barley loaf to her three sick children, was preparing a thin gruel from her last handful of meal which was to suffice for her husband's supper when he came home. Nevertheless, she took pity upon the traveller and poured out the precious contents of the pot, one meagre bowlful, for him. The saint ate gratefully, blessed the woman and the sleeping children huddled in the bed and went on his way.

As she agonised over what to give her husband when he returned from his labours, there was a muffled scuffling outside and a knocking, or rather a dull thumping, at the door. Opening it, she beheld a fat pig with a basket of fruits and vegetables in its mouth. Scarcely had the animal crossed the threshold when it expired and rolled over, exposing its plump belly in such an inviting manner it might well have been descended from one of the animals which appeared to St Peter at Joppa. Recovering from her surprise, the woman then noticed that the children were no longer in the bed. Minutes later, they burst through the door, looking stronger of limb and ruddier of cheek than she had ever known them to be and carrying armfuls of sticks and logs for the fire.

When their father arrived to be greeted by the exquisite aroma of roasting pork, he too bore fresh bread, strong ale and good tidings. As he sat carving wood in the marketplace, hoping to make a few pence for a candlestick or two, a passing nobleman had stopped to admire his work and offered to pay him handsomely if he would undertake to carry out all the woodwork in the noble's new castle. Thereafter his trade prospered, and the couple lived to a comfortable old age but never did they forget to thank the Lord for the bounty they had received in exchange for a tiny bowl of gruel. It has even been said that they opened the original inn on this site to show their gratitude by providing sustenance for weary travellers.

The alternative explanation, favoured by more scholarly types, is that the inn was once called the Holy Grail. The original sign, it is reasonably surmised, depicted that sacred cup with rays of light shining from it. Simple, uneducated folk, knowing nothing of the legendary vessel, saw the image of what looked to them like a dish of steaming porridge, heard that strange phrase the Holy Grail and took it to be the Bowl of Gruel.

The Hump, Epfield

This name recalls another legend concerning the Blessed Witta. It is said that the saint, whilst passing through the village, came across a hunchback being taunted by a group of young men, took pity on him and pronounced him cured of his deformity. To the amazement of the onlookers, no sooner had the words of blessing been uttered than the hump fell from the man's back and lodged in the road. Rebuking the tormentors, Witta warned them never to approach the place again.

Over the years, many superstitions have grown up surrounding the hump in the road. The most common version is that no-one should touch it unless he or she is absolutely pure and sinless for fear of contracting some foul disfigurement. Other variants concern the expected fate of those who mock the afflicted or of murderers, thieves and sundry miscreants, but all are based on the premise that the hump is lying dormant, biding its time until it finds a deserving victim to which to attach itself. Until quite recently, mothers would threaten their children that if they were naughty the hump would get them and any accidents on that stretch of road were routinely attributed to its malign influence.

The Hump
Epfield

Oxbake Brewery Company

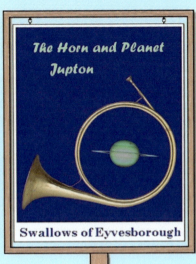

The Horn and Planet
Jupton

Swallows of Eyvesborough

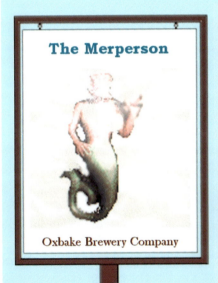

The Merperson

Oxbake Brewery Company

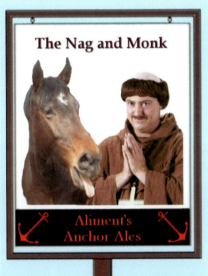

The Nag and Monk

Aliment's
Anchor Ales

Today, villagers will confidently point to a lump in the tarmac some twenty yards west of the pub and tell you that this is the site of the miracle. And most of them won't tread on it - just in case.

The Horn and Planet, Jupton

The origins of this name are lost in antiquity. One vaguely plausible theory is that it is a corruption of "the horned Plantagenet", referring to a local belief that King John was the devil incarnate – and probably born in Oxbake.

The Merperson, Long Dafferd

This name is not an early example of inclusive language. At one time it was definitely "gender specific". However, the pub shut for forty-three years during the nineteenth century. The landlord, a rude and cantankerous old fellow called Ezra Punt, decided one evening in 1839 to close it, threw out his customers (not that there were many, since most of the regulars had long since migrated to the Plough where the ale was not usually sour and drinkers were not subjected to a continuous barrage of verbal abuse) and bolted the door, which remained shut until his death 23 years later.

His son inherited the property and lived there as a recluse until he died in 1882. He never entered the bar which was thick with dust and cobwebs and, it was rumoured, half-empty pint pots still on the tables. On the demise of the younger Punt, Oxbake Brewery Company acquired the building and reopened it. The trouble was, nobody could remember for sure whether it had been the Mermaid or the Merman. A faded sign still hung outside but although the bottom half of the figure depicted thereon was undoubtedly fishy, the androgynous and barely discernible features of the head and upper torso gave no hint as to its gender.

The Mayor of Oxbake, a practical man with a capacity for linguistic philistinism years ahead of his time, suggested it be called the Merperson; the brewery readily agreed and the name was adopted. The sign today is a replica of the faded original.

The Nag and Monk, Shrokeby

Formerly the Nag's Head, this small cosy pub was renamed in affectionate memory of a dyslexic choirmaster.

The Rabbit Pie, Stilchester

This old inn has stood facing the Market Cross since the 16th century. It is a well-known landmark and lends its name to a tram stop. The significance of rabbit pie is that around 1577-8 there was in the city and nearby villages, as reported in the annals of St Cedd's, "a noisome pestilence which hath laid waste ye swine" (probably an outbreak of swine fever). Fortunately, rabbits were plentiful and for a short time superseded pork as the staple diet of the people.

The Railway Tun, Eyvesborough

This sign is dedicated to the work of Josiah Crackling, master cooper at Swallows Brewery from 1896 to 1948. When demand for new casks or repairs was slack, he amused himself building a giant cask; at six feet long and almost four feet in diameter, it had a capacity of 69 cubic feet, equivalent to 12 barrels or two tuns.

When it was finished in September 1925, the parish council of his home town, Kings Pebberworth, asked to have it filled with beer to celebrate Harvest Festival. Swallows were happy to oblige but there was one problem – it was too big to fit on the dray. Then Will Grout, the signalman at Kings Pebberworth, came up with a novel solution. Given its size and shape, the cask would sit neatly on a standard gauge railway line and could be rolled the 14 miles from Eyvesborough to Kings Pebberworth during the night. And so the cask set off on its journey, with ropes looped around its middle towed by two horses and eager volunteers following with lanterns to keep an eye on it and give it a push where necessary.

All was well until halfway up the long incline from Dimley Vale to Prumeford where one of the ropes broke. The startled horse shied and spooked its companion, both bolted and the cask began rolling gently backwards. By the time order had been restored, the cask had travelled nearly two miles in the wrong direction and it was clear that the task would not be completed before morning. Fortunately, with the aid of fresh horses, the cask was rolled into the siding at Prumeford minutes before the 6.30 from Stilchester arrived. The following night the remainder of the journey, now on level ground, was completed without further mishap, the ale still had a few days to settle and the 3,456 pints were duly enjoyed by the townsfolk.

The Little Walrus, Stilhaven

A new pub opened following the re-establishment of Aliment's brewery, it takes its name from strange events which occurred more than a century ago. Early in 1908 a young male walrus was spotted swimming off Gryatt island. For some weeks he remained in the area, at times even venturing into Stilhaven harbour. The following year he returned – and the year after. Strangely he never grew to full size and seemed to prefer the proximity of humans to that of his own species. In due course he became known as "Russell" and was much loved by local children, who would go down to the harbour after school in the hope of seeing him, and fishermen who would feed him any unsalable specimens from their catch.

One stormy afternoon in March 1913 some fishermen heading back to the quay were startled to see Russell alongside their boat, barking and waving his flippers agitatedly. Eventually convinced that he was trying to tell them something, they turned the boat around and followed the walrus who was now swimming determinedly towards the harbour mouth. Despite the foul weather and the treacherous currents, they continued to follow him beyond Sowport into the open water – and there they saw a small lifeboat tossing alarmingly in the turbulent waves. Hastening towards it, they found six terrified children cowering inside. With some difficulty they were able to transfer the young castaways into their own boat and return to the safety of the harbour with Russell swimming behind.

It later transpired that a pleasure boat, the SS Marchioness of Eyvesborough, on a day trip from Crachelton-on-Sea, had run into difficulties when the storm blew up. The crew had deployed the lifeboats, putting the children into the first one, but before a crew member could join them the vessel lurched suddenly, the cables snapped and the lifeboat was swiftly swept away. Mercifully, no lives were lost, the steamer having run aground at Stiltmouth with everyone remaining on board until the storm abated, and the children were none the worse for their ordeal.

Russell was the hero of the day. He continued to be seen around Stilhaven for many years and when he failed to return in 1934, having presumably died of natural causes, a statue was erected in his memory on the quay.

The Inn Sign Inn, Gerbelton

This is not an old inn; it was built in the 1920s. At the time there was some dispute over the naming of it, there being one faction that wished it to be called The Rampant Ram or Tuppence Halfpenny, after a prize specimen of ovine masculinity of that name who had recently died, whilst another group favoured the more prosaic Gerbelton Arms. While the protagonists argued the merits of their respective nomenclatures, the pub opened and the brewery erected a temporary sign bearing the legend "Inn Sign" and the brewery logo. Some weeks into the protracted dispute, it became apparent to the landlord, who had determined not to take sides, that regulars and visitors alike were beginning to refer to the place as "The Inn Sign". Gradually the debate subsided with neither side emerging victorious and the adopted name stuck.

It was at this point that the local artist and mathematician Augustus Steed, at the behest of the landlord, produced a splendid new inn sign depicting an inn sign depicting an inn sign depicting an inn sign depicting an inn sign depicting an inn sign depicting an inn sign depicting an inn sign depicting an inn sign depicting an inn sign depicting an inn sign depicting an inn sign depicting an inn sign depicting an inn sign depicting an inn sign depicting an inn sign depicting an inn sign depicting an inn sign depicting an inn sign depicting ……

This is believed to be the only recursive inn sign in the world. The current version, now becoming a little faded, has 37 nested iterations of the design, eight more than Steed's original. A local man who runs a computer aided design company has offered to make a replacement which he claims will have at least 1000 iterations and the landlord is considering augmenting his profits by hiring step ladders and magnifying glasses to those who wish to verify the claim for themselves.

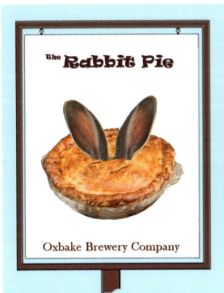

The **Rabbit Pie**

Oxbake Brewery Company

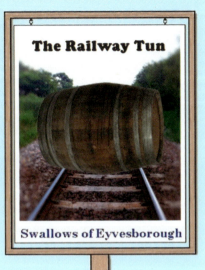

The Railway Tun

Swallows of Eyvesborough

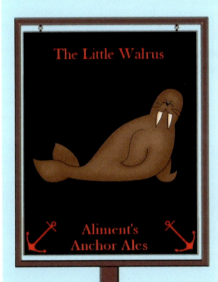

The Little Walrus

Aliment's
Anchor Ales

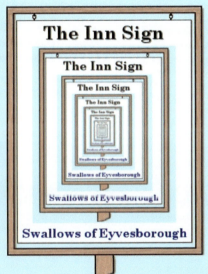

The Inn Sign

Swallows of Eyvesborough

Songs of Stiltshire

Folk Singing

The art of folk singing thrives in Stiltshire. Whenever two or three singers are gathered together in a public house, they are likely to give a rendering of their county's traditional songs and ballads and perchance even some of their own compositions in the genre.

Sometimes these are impromptu performances, sometimes regular events like Friday nights at the Black Sheep in Lower Pebberworth, where the best exponents of the art may be heard, either *a capella* or accompanied by fiddle, melodeon and the peculiar double-barrelled hurdy-gurdy. In the livelier numbers, people may improvise a gentle percussion by clicking their tongues or by "clackling" with the shoulder-blades of a suckling pig played in the manner of spoons or castanets.

Notable contemporary musicians include the Dongland singer Sally Medlar-Bell, daughter of the late hurdy-gurdy maker Phineas Bell, Somerset Pine, founder of the local record label Ruckworth Pepper Records (although his own musical career has lately deviated into some rather bizarre musical forms), and the highly acclaimed folk-rock band Blivet Eye.

Dafferd Down

This doleful dirge is often accompanied on the hurdy-gurdy. Alternate verses may be sung to a counter-melody, which is a mirror image of the main melody.

Walking o'er Dafferd Down one Autumn morning,
Cold was the air as the grey light a-dawning.

High above Cruftmere, where lately I sleep-ed,
Came I upon a grave, fresh sod an-heap-ed.

Down toward Epfield, my measured tread keeping,
Saw I a fair maid lay on the ground weeping.

Tell me my pretty one, why weepst thou sorely?
Thy tears would water the Forest of Knorrley.

Tis for a young man, alas slain in battle.
The brown leaves they shake like my true love's death rattle.

Homeward I wandered and sadly I mus-ed,
Ofttimes are beauty and promise abus-ed.

[instrumental interlude]

Walking o'er Dafferd Down one fair Spring morning,
Green buds unfolding and brown frogs a-spawning.

High above Cruftmere, where late I had slumbered,
A low mossy mound with primroses unnumbered.

Down toward Epfield, the wind softly sighing,
A pair of young lovers upon a bank lying.

'Twas that same pretty maid, once lay a-weeping,
Now in a new love's arms, peacefully sleeping.

Though Autumn be dreary and Winter be meaner,
Next year the grass on the grave groweth greener.

Oft when it seemeth life is but sorrow,
'Tis then the sun beameth brighter the morrow.

[The song traditionally ends with the hurdy-gurdy players hastily retuning their instruments to effect a tierce-de-Picardie.]

Aiden o' Skent

This version of an old Stiltshire ballad was collected by Rev'd Ezra Rhodes from a farmer at Trome in 1911. In the annals of the Worshipful Company of Sievewrights there are several references to an itinerant musician called Aiden of Skent who apparently lived from about 1660 to 1730 and, although the song uses the mildly derogatory term "organ grinder", it seems probable that he was actually a skilled performer on the Stiltshire hurdy-gurdy. The fourth verse is to be chanted, Anglican-style, loosely following the notes of the tune; some performers embellish it with phrases of their own to make the lines even longer.

It's of a jolly organ grinder,
Tripped o'er the hills with his monkey, Ken.
Tuned up his pipes with a big brass winder,
Played for the plebs and the noblemen.
Played all the day in the harvest field,
Seven fold increased the yield,
All night long in the local inn
Ceaseless his music he reeled.

Month after month did the organ grinder
Churn out his notes on the village green.
Monkey got up on his legs, the hinder,
Danced for pauper and danced for queen.
Aiden o' Skent was the grinder's name,
Far 'cross Stiltshire spread his fame,
Ladies swooned and the children's eyen
Sparkled wherever he came.

Year after year did the trusty Aiden
Ply his trade in the market square.
Ken capered high for crone and maiden,
Bowed and curtsied with noble air.
Played for the Bishop at the Chapter Ball,
Played for the Mayor in the Sievewrights' Hall.
High on the Drones and the hill tops bare
Played for nobody at all.

One bitterly cold winter's night in the Bowl of Gruel inn on the | square at |
Prokeworth
Poor little monkey Ken caught a dreadful chill and | on the | morrow he | died.
Aiden o' Skent, dealt this blow so cruel, in deep despair, his | poor heart | broke,
"Worth
-less am I among men, dealt this fate so ill" in | deepest | sorrow he | cried.
Sadly and slowly he turn-ed the handle of his barrel organ, a | doleful | dirge to
in|voke,
But nought came forth from its bowels but a puff of wind and a | feeble | croak.
Faithful monkey, his life breath spent, and faithful organ, its bellows rent, were laid
to rest side by side in the shade | of a | mighty | oak,
And wretched Aiden o' Skent, though he lived out his three score years and ten,
yet never more a note he | played nor a | word he | spoke.

Now, rest ye assured, in the Courts of Heaven,
Man and monkey together dwell,
Dance and play on the barrel organ
To souls redeemed from the flames of Hell.
Play for the Seraphim on bended knees,
Play for St Peter with his brace of keys,
Play to the might and the majesty
Of the Blessed Trinity.

The Banks of Clover

'Twas by the banks of clover
My love did walk with me,
From Cowpole down to Flover
And over Hakeford lea.
To me her troth she plighted
That buxom, red-head maid,
And I was well delighted
As in my arms she laid.

We took a house in Flover
Close by the Priory gate
And there it first behove her
To live in wedlock's state.
Yet ne'er would I have wagered,
Ere six months we were wed,
A handsome Sergeant Major'd
Have turned her pretty head.

Then often would I wander
Through old Stilhaven town,
And all my money squander
My sorrows for to drown.
One night in spirits sunken
A-lying on the quay,
All sick, forlorn and drunken,
An idea came to me.

Next morn I found a clipper
Was leaving for Bombay,
And told the jovial skipper
I'd work for modest pay.
And thus I joined the sailors
Who cross the ocean wide,
And left my cares and failures
Upon the ebbing tide.

'Twas seven long years after
When home I came on leave
Now filled with mirth and laughter,
I long had ceased to grieve.
A-drinking in the Mermaid
With comrades of the crew,
My eye lit on the barmaid,
A face that well I knew.

She cried she'd been mistaken,
By uniform beguiled.
He'd left her all forsaken
When great she was with child.

If I could but forgive her
And go to sea no more,
She'd cook me tripe and liver
And stray not from my door.

I told my faithless lover
"I am a sailor bold.
Tis too late to recover
The love we had of old.
I'll roam the whole world over,
I'll sail the western sea,
And never think of Flover
Nor shed one tear for thee."

The Boar and the Sow

Now down Flinton way an old farmer did dwell,
And kept he his pigs there as many knew well.
At Pebberworth market one fine summer day
For a young Prumeford sow he a guinea did pay.
And it's drink to the farm boys who follow the plough,
And it's drink to the goodwife, the boar and the sow.

This sow was called Hannah and pleased the old boy.
She was just like a daughter, his pride and his joy.
He fed her on parsnips to fatten her out,
And each night he brought her a gallon of stout.
And it's…

Now down around Flinton sweet parsnips abound,
And fed on this diet she grew fat and round.
In truth she did measure a yard round the head,
And so broad in the beam she got stuck in the shed.
And it's…

Then th'old farmer's missus she leaned on the gate
And said "Tis high time yon fat sow had a mate.
There's a boar down the lane as'd suit her just fine,
And bring us a litter of cute little swine."
And it's…

The boar was a big 'un, his bristles stood up,
And he went to the field like a ram to the tup,
But, seeing that mighty sow, trembled alack,
Went weak at the knees and fell flat on his back.
And it's…

Still Hannah grew wider and wider until
She looked like a pumpkin or Witterspool Hill.
Though many more suitors were brought to her door,
They quailed at the sight of her, just like before.
And it's...

Now over at Trome lived a prize Smoatham boar,
Who'd sired a few piglets, nine hundred or more.
His tackle was awesome, a sight to behold,
And they called him Zerubbabel, the fearless and bold.
And it's...

Zerubbabel he stood on the old village green,
A beast so majestic there seldom was seen.
And the farmer brought Hannah and walked by her side,
While the wheezy church organ played "Here comes the bride".
And it's...

The boar's eyes did water and Heavenward swerve,
So they gave him a brandy to stiffen his nerve.
Then the good folk of Flinton averted their gaze,
And left the two pigs to their nuptial ways.
And it's...

Zerubbabel he's altered, his wild oats long sown,
With big homely Hannah he's now settled down.
And the good folk of Flinton need have no more fears,
There'll be plenty of bacon to last them for years.
And it's drink to the farm boys who follow the plough,
And it's drink to the goodwife, the boar and the sow.

Biddy Bullock's Brawn

Oh, when I was a tiny boy
It used to be my greatest joy
To sit at Biddy Bullock's knee,
Eyes wide open, for to see
Th'old girl making brawn.

Now, first she'd take a great pig's
head
From out the brine tub, whence 't
had bled,
She'd scrub the ears and then the
nose
Pink and spotless as a rose
For Biddy Bullock's brawn.

The old black pan to do the job
Was set a-simmering on the hob,
With clear spring water, freshly
drawn,
Blade of mace and peppercorn
For Biddy Bullock's brawn.

Of lemon balm she'd take a sprig,
Of garden thyme a little twig,
Parsley, sage and bay leaves three,
Ah, the smell was heavenly
Of Biddy Bullock's brawn.

Then, when the boiling was
complete,
She'd pick the bones and chop the
meat,
And pack it into basins four,
Let them cool beside the door
For Biddy Bullock's brawn.

Upon each one she'd set a plate
And, top of that, a five pound
weight,
For else the jelly wouldn't press,
'Twould be instead a sloppy mess
Not Biddy Bullock's brawn.

Next day you'd see old Bid and me
Sat in the parlour taking tea,
Of fresh brown bread a goodly hunk
And on the top a great thick chunk
Of Biddy Bullock's brawn.

In all my life I've travelled free
To distant lands beyond the sea,
And tasted dishes strange and rare,
But none there be than can compare
With Biddy Bullock's brawn

Grittersham Fell

Grittersham Fell is the second highest peak in the North Drones, the highest being Slack Tor. Although it affords spectacular views on a sunny day, it can be a bleak, miserable place in winter. Clearly it offered no comfort to the young lady in the ballad, whose lover is dead, having apparently committed some heinous and unforgiveable crime (cf. "Dafferd Down" and "Whenever the Cowslips").

Grey falls the rain o'er Grittersham Fell,
The streamlets in torrents flowing.
Then hangs o'er the dell a dank Autumn smell,
And cattle a-sadly lowing.

Cold blows the wind o'er Grittersham Fell,
The boughs of the pine trees swaying.
Then sounds a lone bell, my lover's death knell,
And I on my knees a-praying.

White lays the snow o'er Grittersham Fell,
The small birds on branches freezing.
Then my heart can tell his soul lies in Hell
And naught for his torment's easing.

Fresh drops the dew o'er Grittersham Fell,
The earth wakes from Winter's sleeping.
Then tears they do swell and my heart knows well
That Spring brings no more but weeping.

The Old Churchyard

It's of the rogue who ne'er atones,
He plied his trade on the North Drones.
He was tried and hung from the gallows hard
And they buried him in the old churchyard.

The evil warlock of Domewell,
Upon the stake, sent down to Hell,
His body burned, his organs charred
And they buried him in the old churchyard.

The killers three of Spruntley Moor,
Who spilled the blood of thirty four,
The axeman's blow was their reward
And they buried them in the old churchyard.

So keep the precepts of thy Lord,
Be plenty fearful of his word,
Lest you be put to the justice sword,
And you'll sleep unsound in the old churchyard.

The "old churchyard" is that of St. Decimus, Everbone. Deconsecrated in 1742, when the new church of St Audrey opened, it was used for nearly two centuries for the burial of murderers and other felons. [see also the Miraculous Frying Pan.]

"The rogue who ne'er atones" was Jacob Bezzle, a notorious footpad, sheep rustler and desecrator of churches who carried out his nefarious deeds among the hills of North Stiltshire for two decades until he was finally caught and brought to justice in February 1743. As he stood on the gallows, he refused the last rites, dismissing the priest with a torrent of abuse. For this he was denied a Christian burial and became the first criminal to be buried in the old churchyard.

He was soon joined by Newton Mordford, the "warlock of Domewell", whose charred corpse *had hung in a rusting gibbet at the boundaries of Domewell, Everbone and Britlam for almost 50 years because no parish would accept it. Mordford was by all accounts a thoroughly wicked, amoral and manipulative man who may or may not have possessed supernatural powers but certainly exerted a sinister influence over his small band of followers, whom he compelled to commit acts of unspeakable depravity. When, in 1688, the Vicar died in mysterious circumstances, no cleric could be found man enough to replace him. For seven years the population of Domewell lived in terror of the warlock, suspicious of their neighbours, averting their gaze, stopping their ears and keeping silent lest they be next to fall under his evil eye. Eventually Mordford's downfall was brought about through the bravery of two children: when he demanded of a young couple that they give up their infant son for sacrifice, the child's brother and sister witnessed the entire grisly ceremony through a hole in the ceiling and reported what they had seen to a priest. Several of the coven were hanged, others imprisoned, and the warlock burnt at the stake and then (some say he was not yet dead) consigned to his lonely cage in no man's land.*

The "killers three of Spruntley Moor" were vicious highwaymen, who held up coaches or solitary travellers on the lonely Spruntley to Stiltford road or the Epfield Turnpike and claimed 31 lives in as many months before being tracked down to their hideaway in Knorrley Forest by an elite squad of the Marquess of Eyvesborough's private army. In the ensuing battle, three soldiers and two of the highwaymen were killed, the other being summarily tried and executed within a few days.

Oxbake Ale

This song was written in 1903 by the Oxbake poet, singer, toper and otherwise good-for-nothing, Alan Bletwood. Listening to the six bells of St Benedict's church ringing the Queen's change one day whilst waiting for opening time, it seemed to him that they were calling "Oxbake Ale, Oxbake Ale". Musicians and ringers may be interested to note that the fifth bell is 13lb heavier, and therefore more sonorous, than the Tenor, the latter being a very ancient and thin bell. This is presumably why the sound inspired Bletwood to write a tune in the minor key, rather than in the major with the Tenor note as the tonic.

The words attribute many strange happenings to the powers of the local brew, including the disastrous storm which destroyed the Jupton harvest in 1837 (though most of the county was unscathed). Since Bletwood's time, other verses have been added, including the references to Harry Bromley and the (probably fictitious) balloonist, Ted Mountnimbus.

Chorus:
Oxbake Ale, Oxbake Ale,
Makes you stout and makes you hale.
Old or bitter, mild or porter,
Drink it oft instead of water.
Thus refreshed you'll never fail.

Farmhands after harvest thirsting,
Drank two gallons of Best apiece,
Wandered homeward, bladders bursting,
Wondering where to find release.
To the Smithy hopped the members
Of that gallant farmyard team,
Gathered round the glowing embers,
Put up a mighty cloud of steam.

All that night there fell on Jupton
Rain in torrents thick and fast,
Didn't bother Thrimp or Strupton,
Over Wizards Alton passed.
All night long on Jupton's rooftops,
Biggest rain since Noah's flood,
Washed away the stooks and haycocks,
Turned their cornfields into mud.
Chorus

Harry Bromley in the choir at
Stilchester the bass part sang.
Fifty years his bottom B flat
Round the ancient pillars rang.
Harry swore by Apster's daughter,

Never wavered from this stance,
'Twas daily quarts of Oxbake Porter
Gave it extra resonance.
Chorus

Giovanni Giacometti,
Engineer beyond compare,
With his heart on Oxbake set, he
Said "I'll build a railway there".
But alas, to Spruntley town.
Giovanni's railway never got.
Oxbake station twice burnt down
And no more money in the pot.

Oxbake folk were sad and rueful,
Seeing his dream go down the drain.
And besides, if they were truthful,
Would've liked to go by train.
"But" they said, not really jestful,
"Foreigners are bound to fail.
If you want to be successful
You should drink more Oxbake
Ale".
Chorus

Brother James on St Magg's Island
Knelt within his hermit's cell,
Visions of the Heavenly high land
Marred by torturous dreams of Hell,
Till he at last in desperation
Sent for casks of Oxbake Old.
Now in blissful contemplation
Dwells he in that blessed abode.
Chorus

Ted Mountnimbus, ace balloonist
Took off one morn from Wittering
Reed.
Burner flared and hot air soon hissed,
Up he went with grace and speed.
Half mile high disaster struck,
Of heat and flame a sudden dearth,
All because a valve had stuck.
Balloon did plummet back to earth.

Undeterred, th' intrepid Edward
Broached a bottle of Oxbake Light,
Drank it down and, head turned
upward,
Huffed and puffed with all his might.
Balloon no longer hurtled earthward,
Floated gently on the breeze,
Came to rest in Quisham churchyard
By a clump of rowan trees.
Chorus

Oxbake bells, so say the people,
Are a noble ring and loud,
And atop the little steeple
Stands a weathercock so proud.
Once the ringers rang a peal
To celebrate the Jubilee.
On the tenor, Reuben Kneale
Conducted it most skilfully.

Half way through his voice grew
hoarse,
A little fainter with each call.
Time they'd rung another course
He couldn't make a sound at all.
Weathercock, with speed
astounding,
Down into the chamber flew,
Called the bobs and brought the peal
round,
"That's all. Stand" triumphant crew.

Second ringer wasn't local.
"That" he said "was quite absurd.
How can you get calls so vocal
From a copper-plated bird?"
So they told the chap from
Cruftmere
How the cock could sing so fine.
Each time steeple-keeper's up there,
He gives him a nip of barley wine.
Chorus

Lavender Lea

'Twas down by the harbour she first took my eye,
As comely a maid as I e'er did espy.
The sun set blood red o'er the boats on the sea
When I met my true love at Stilhaven Quay.

With cherry red lips, and long tresses of gold,
Young Lavender Lea was a sight to behold.
That night, she her maidenhead gave unto me,
And long will I love my dear Lavender Lea.

The months swiftly passed, like a jug of good mild,
And soon my dear Lavender grew plump with child.
But a poor fisher's son, I could ne'er buy a ring,
And my true love was taken to Lower Ryming.

I joined the King's navy my fortune to seek
And sailed the salt seas for a year and a week.
I'd gold in my pocket and hope in my heart
That I and my Lavender ne'er more should part.

But e'en as my ship homeward sailed from the Cape
From Ryming's grim madhouse she'd made her escape.
And as we sailed back into Stilhaven Quay
My love on the dockside knelt weeping for me.

When many a tear she had shed for my sake,
She cried for the Good Lord her soul for to take.
With the babe in her arms she leapt into the brine,
Alas, that she knew not that the tall ship was mine.

Though I cross the far ocean and plough the deep sea,
I'll never forget my sweet Lavender Lea,
For all this wide world is as nothing to me
Since I lost my true love at Stilhaven Quay.

A byword for shame and disgrace during the 18th and 19th centuries, Lower Ryming Hospital was an asylum to which "fallen women" were often sent, as well as the mentally disturbed.

Passing Gryatt

For many generations of Stiltshire mariners, Gryatt Island opposite Stilhaven Harbour was the last and, if they were lucky, the first sight of their homeland. In this poignant ballad, the sailor thinks wistfully of his childhood haunts and asks his true love to remember him in his absence. Note the use of "piglet" as a typical term of endearment.

Fare thee well, my dear piglet and God keep thee sound,
For I am passing of Gryatt on a tall ship outbound,
Ploughing into the mighty and merciless sea,
Far away from my homeland and further from thee.
Hang down, hang down thy chestnut brown hair
And weep for me, oh my true love, my blossom so fair.

In the passing of Gryatt I've shed many tears
O'er Chineham's sweet orchards and Wilberton's meres,
For the friends of my childhood and fields of my home,
For the steeple at Prokeworth and Lydegar's dome.
Hang down, hang down thy chestnut brown hair
And think of me on the ocean whilst thou art still there.

If the Good Lord preserve me and spare me death's pain,
May it fall to my lot to pass Gryatt again,
Then a-landward returning to Stilhaven quay,
Over Kibblebrook's meadows and then homeward to thee.
Hang down, hang down thy chestnut brown hair
And welcome me to thy bosom, my jewel so rare.

The Sievewright and the Swineherd

In Aggerby glade there dwelt a maid
Of beauty matched by few
And to place a band on her dainty hand
Was the aim of suitors two.
With a vol-de-rol tiddle taddle tong, me boys,
was the aim of suitors two.

Now young Sam Griggs kept the squire's pigs
In the fields of Clabworth Lea
And whistling Ron came from Narkington
And a master sievewright he.
With a vol-de-rol tiddle taddle tong, me boys,
and a master sievewright he.

'Twas at Whitsun fete by the churchyard gate
Bespake that fair young maid:
"I'll pledge my hand and wed the man
That plies the worthier trade."
With a vol-de-rol tiddle taddle tong, me boys,
that plies the worthier trade.

So the swineherd averred: "I keep my herd
From harm and danger free,
'Til the butcher's knife shall take their life
For a Sunday joint for thee."
With a vol-de-rol tiddle taddle tong, me boys,
for a Sunday joint for thee.

And the sievewright spake: "My sieves I make
Full of myriad tiny holes,
That the flour so rough shall be finer stuff,
As pure as infant souls."
With a vol-de-rol tiddle taddle tong, me boys,
as pure as infant souls.

Then the maid's eyes rolled, "'Twixt hogs and holes
I swear I can't decide.
Let the strongest man of the bravest clan
Come take me for his bride."
With a vol-de-rol tiddle taddle tong, me boys,
come take me for his bride.

Then, lo and behold, a grenadier bold
Came a-riding down the street.
At the maid so spry he wink-ed his eye
As he swept her off her feet.
With a vol-de-rol tiddle taddle tong, me boys,
as he swept her off her feet.

Through the sievewright's thoughts and the swineherd's naught
But the words of the psalmist ran:
"Put not your trust in princesses
Nor in any child of man."
With a vol-de-rol tiddle taddle tong, me boys,
nor in any child of man.

So the pair took flight, as any men might
When their hopes and dreams do fail,
To the Rose and Crown, their woes to drown
And to drink their fill of ale.
With a vol-de-rol tiddle taddle tong, me boys,
and to drink their fill of ale.

Sir Roderick Snebwood

This notorious minor aristocrat became, despite his eleventh-hour repentance, something of a bogeyman in Stiltshire folklore. [See the Haunted Pulpit.]

Sir Roderick Snebwood rode out on a day
And ne'er went he to the church to pray.
He rode o'er moorland, o'er field and fell,
Nor cared he aught for the flames of Hell.

As he rode westward and he rode east,
He shewed no mercy to man nor beast.
Full threescore horses he rode to death,
And flogged them all to their dying breath.

Of meat and liquor he took his fill.
Of divers women he had his will.
There's seventeen maidens now mothers be
And seven died for their modesty.

And when he hear-ed the scriptures taught,
He shot the parson e'en as he praught.
And as he pray-ed, that pastor good,
He lay a-dying in his own blood.

Sir Roderick Snebwood, for that foul deed,
He must be punished it was decreed.
So he was sentenced forthwith to die
And hanged was on the gallows high.

And when he passeth the gates of Hell,
There's seven maidens shall ring the bell.
His torment needeth not wheel nor rack;
There's threescore horses shall break his back.

Sir Roderick Snebwood rode out on a day
And ne'er went he to the church to pray.
He rode o'er moorland, o'er field and fell
And now he burns in the flames of Hell.

Whenever the Cowslips

This song was sung to Rev'd Ezra Rhodes by a milkmaid at Hazzock, who did not include the penultimate verse. She may have felt intimidated by the dog collar - the verse was commonly sung by several female vocalists in the area during the 1930s, so is probably authentic.

Whenever the cowslips do bloom I'll remember my love
And the green fields of Hazedale where oft in the evening we'd rove,
With the scent of the hay stacks, the warmth as I lay by his side
And the music of laughter and bitter sweet tears that we cried.

One night as he drank with his friends at the Marquess's Head,
A terrible fight did ensue with two men left for dead.
He was taken and tried for their blood had been found on his knife
And to far Australia my love was transported for life.

I married a blacksmith, a good man, stout hearted and true,
But his touch never thrilled me the way that my old love could do.
I had four sturdy children and now they've got babes of their own,
But sometimes I still feel a young maid bereft and alone.

And sometimes while sleeping my soul soars across the deep sea
To the shores of Australia, where my love lies waiting for me.
And I daren't tell the priest for I'm sure he would deem it a sin,
But that's where this false world doth end and the real one begin.

Whenever the cowslips do bloom I'll remember my love
And the green fields of Hazedale where oft in the evening we'd rove.
And when mine eyes dim and my old limbs will bear me no more,
My love will be waiting there for me on yonder bright shore.

The White Silk Gown

Beyond yon forest dark and wide dwelleth a maid in a white silk gown.
I saw her once at eventide, under the hill where the stream runs down.

Her skin was pale as is the moon. Fair was that maid in the white silk gown.
Her dainty feet wore crystal shoon, under the hill where the stream runs down.

Her hair was black as raven's wing, gently it fell o'er the white silk gown.
And oh, how sweetly she did sing, under the hill where the stream runs down.

"Oh wilt thou come away with me, beautiful maid in the white silk gown?
This day we two might married be" under the hill where the stream runs down.

She cast on me a fleeting smile, did the fair maid in the white silk gown,
Whose rosebud lips my heart beguile, under the hill where the stream runs down.

"Oh would that I might go with thee", sighed the fair maid in the white silk gown.
"I must stay here for eternity under the hill where the stream runs down".

"Life is a cup that will not last", soft sang the maid in the white silk gown.
"So drink it soon, e'er it be past", under the hill where the stream runs down.

Ah, then I was a young man bold, thrall to that maid in the white silk gown.
Long years have passed and now I'm old, over the hill where the stream runs down.

And still that music haunts me yet, song of the maid in the white silk gown.
Her heavenly face I'll ne'er forget, under the hill where the stream runs down.

Perchance that, when my hour shall come, then the fair maid in the white silk gown
Will take my hand and lead me home, under the hill where the stream runs down.

Wild Garlic

This song has been known to generations of folk singers as "Wild Garlic" for reasons which are not entirely clear, apart from the passing reference in verse two, though it surely evokes the rolling clifftops and woodlands between Blefton and Fruspool where in May the evening air is redolent with the scent of wild garlic.

Every line ends with the consonant 'n', and the singer traditionally closes her mouth on the final slurred note of each line to produce a kind of humming sound.

On clifftops high I shade mine eye 'gainst the rays of the setting su'n,
And my feet might skip should there e'er be a ship, though my poor heart desires but o'ne.
But in calm or in gale there's never a sail for my love will no more retur'n
And like the salt sea the tears well in me and cold on my cheeks they bur'n.

As daylight fades I walk the glades with scent of wild garlic lade'n.
Its frail flowers white re-echo the plight of a lost and forsaken maide'n.
And above the dank caves the bluebells in waves all their sad little heads droop dow'n,
And on that deep I'd lay me to sleep; oh, would that I there might drow'n.

Stilhaven Quay

This is probably an old seafarers' melody (the sort of thing that was played on the concertina to encourage the tars while winding the capstan) which at some point, no doubt with the help of rum or ale, became married to a mariner's tall tale. There are other, equally preposterous, versions of the words.

Oh, we left the Six Bells and our ship we did board
And from Stilhaven Quay we set sail.
We'd all bid our farewells to the girls we adored
And we'd sunk a few gallons of ale.

It was late afternoon and St Magg's far astern,
When a strange looking bird we did spy.
It was pale as the moon and its green eyes did burn
And straight over our mast it did fly.

Then the sky it turned black and the wind it did roar,
And the vessel spun round like a top.
When a whirlpool appeared spitting brimstone and gore
And right into its maw did we drop.

Then the ship turned around and so swiftly it sped
Through a tunnel whose walls shone like ice,
And all through the long night the strange bird flew ahead
While we cowered as quiet as mice.

Till at last we saw light and the good ship shot forth
Like a ball from a great cannon gun,
And it flew o'er the hills and encircled the earth
And went damn near half way to the sun.

When at length it came down in an ocean so wide
For a month the horizon we scanned,
Till the first mate looked down from the crow's nest and cried
"Ahoy! I see land! I see land!"

Then our Captain looked out and a wise man was he
Threescore years o'er the globe he did roam.
"By St Ewburga's bones, 'tis New Zealand!" quoth he,
"Me fine lads, we're a long way from home."

After weeks of no victuals, no rum and no ale
We sailed back into Stilhaven Quay,
And we drank and we sang and oft told we our tale
But no man would believe it of we.

Mong Music

In the west of Dongland are nine hills, known as the Eyt Mongs and the Greyt Mong, and this area is home to a unique style of singing known as Mong Music. There are always nine singers, each one associated with one of the hills, spanning the entire compass of the human vocal range from an ethereally high soprano (Pipit Mong) to basso profundo (Greyt Mong). Typically, they will have grown up in the villages of Hippleton Mercy and Hippleton Grace or somewhere close by and parts are often handed down through generations of the same family.

The music itself is a kind of vocalese or song without words, although the tradition goes back many centuries and there is a persistent belief that some of the oldest songs are actually ballads in a long-forgotten local language. Indeed, Dr Thomas Thanks of the University of Brinceton, who spent many years researching the history of Mong Music, came up with the following interpretation of the song *Ob si Narrum*:

"The exuberant arpeggios in the soprano parts at the beginning imitate the twittering of birds in the branches and the fluttering of butterflies, while the gently undulating baritone represents the lowing of placid cattle. Short staccato phrases in the alto suggest the scurrying of small creatures, the whole underpinned by a soft drone redolent of a sleepy Summer's day. Then the sudden entry of two tenor voices in an alien key heralds the arrival of a pair of fearsome goblins from the sea. For a while chaos and discord reign, until a low D flat from Greyt Mong, gradually increasing in volume, betokens the Spirit of the Earth arising to banish the goblins and restore calm, bringing the piece to a harmonious conclusion."

Detractors will say that the music merely evokes the mood of the story, as in an orchestral tone poem. But Dr Thanks insisted that he had decoded much of the ancient language, although he failed to complete his planned dictionary and papers found after his death in 1986 offer little to support the claim. Be that as it may, many of the songs are undoubtedly of great antiquity and each generation adds one or two new ones to the repertory.

In recent years the tradition was thrown into disarray when the Greyt Mong, George Breadth, died suddenly without having groomed a successor. There being no obvious replacement, in desperation the Mong Counsel approached Quainton Rhodes, the well-known bass lay clerk at Stilchester Cathedral, and invited him to join the group. Mr Rhodes replied that, whilst he was very flattered to be asked, he did not really have the time to devote to it and urged them not to break with centuries of tradition. He offered instead to help them find and train a young, local bass for the role and after three weeks' searching among the schools and choirs of Dongland the perfect candidate was located.

At 15, Edward Lung already had an impressive contra-C and his range would undoubtedly deepen with age*. He lived in Brinceton, his family had been in the area for generations and, if that were not qualification enough, his great-grandmother had been Pipit Mong. The lad had a phenomenal memory too and within months was performing the ancient songs as if they were in his bones – which they probably were, or at least in his genes. Thanks to Mr Rhodes' influence, Edward was later offered a scholarship to read music at St Cedd's and a lay clerk's post at the Cathedral, where he now sings alongside his mentor as well as fulfilling his duties as Greyt Mong.

* At the last count he was regularly hitting A flat. Dr Ashley Pencil, the Cathedral's Master of Music, has reputedly taken to composing Russian-style liturgical music, now having two outstanding *oktavisti* in his choir.

Folk Dancing

The Maids of St Enoch are a female dance troupe from the Dongland village of that name who can trace their origins back to the 12th century. At one time the only musical accompaniment was the singing of the dancers themselves and, although the concertina, fiddle and hurdy-gurdy are now used and have been for 200 years, certain dances are still performed *a capella*.

Morris dancing is enormously popular in Stiltshire with many towns and villages fielding a side. The annual Morris Competition is sponsored alternately by Oxbake Brewery and Swallows of Eyvesborough, who of course benefit handsomely from the regular practice of the art at their pubs. [There have been a few anxious moments in the odd year when Jupton have reached the final in an Oxbake-sponsored year, as happened in 2006, but fortunately the organisers had the foresight to invite Aliments to provide a few barrels as well.]

A history of dancing in the county was written by the veteran morrisman A L Harrows (1902-2004) who danced with the Trome side for 89 years and was Squire for 70 of them.

Supernatural Stiltshire

Most Stiltshire folk are of the firm opinion that there is more to life (and death) than meets the eye. This other-worldliness manifests itself not only in a higher than average church attendance but also in a tendency to observe ancient rites and superstitions - and a plethora of tales of the weird, the creepy and the downright bizarre.

Some ghosts are benevolent, harmlessly re-enacting scenes from long ago, some terrifying and some downright malicious, but the accolade for the most tedious ghost in existence must surely go to that which haunts St David's church, Smoatham.

A small town on the banks of the Stilt, Smoatham is a maze of narrow streets with shops which have largely escaped the ravages of progress. The church stands close to the river, a handsome white stone building with a tall tower atop which four elegantly curved buttresses converge into a lantern supporting a thin graceful spire. Inside, the nave is lofty and narrow, flanked by two side aisles and furnished with dark wood, including a very fine pulpit of the Jacobean period. It was here that Isaiah Wenton was instituted as vicar in 1777. A sober minister of the evangelical tendency, the Rev'd Wenton was true to his name; he would preach for two and three quarter hours on an average Sunday, half as long again at festivals.

Now the local squire at that time was Sir Roderick Snebwood, a second cousin of the Snebwoods of Pebberworth Manor and regarded by them as the black sheep of the family. A man of choleric disposition, prone to sudden changes of mood, he was not greatly liked by the townsfolk either. There had been an unpleasant incident a few years earlier when he had flogged a gamekeeper to within an inch of his life, over the trivial matter of the poor man having given a lame pheasant to his unemployed brother-in-law, and he reputedly escaped retribution only by virtue of his habit of regularly entertaining the justices with good claret, game and port wine. He enjoyed the pleasures of the chase at every conceivable opportunity and was notoriously hard on his horses.

On All Souls day, 1792, the office of Matins proceeded much as it did on any other Sunday. At about a quarter to noon, the vicar ascended the pulpit to begin a lengthy discourse on the life of the prophet Jeremiah. For the next hour and fifty minutes, the only sounds apart from the drone of his voice were the occasional subdued coughs and sniffs of his flock and a restless shuffling of feet from the squire's pew. Then, without warning, Sir Roderick sprang to his feet, crying "I have had enough of your prating, Sir!", pulled a pistol from his breeches and discharged it. Now, those who witnessed the action testified that he fired into the air with an extravagant flourish, rather than taking careful aim; indeed, it may have been that he never intended to pull the trigger at all. Be that as it may, the bullet left the muzzle travelling unerringly in the direction of the pulpit.

The echo of the gunshot died away and there was a deathly silence for a moment. Then, amid the shouts, sobs and screams of the congregation, the churchwardens rushed to the aid of their incumbent who was now recumbent in a pool of blood. Fearing the worst, they ascended the steps to find he had sustained a flesh wound to the shoulder. After breathing heavily for a couple of minutes, the vicar struggled to his feet, murmuring "Father, forgive them …", clapped his handkerchief to his bleeding shoulder and resumed the delivery of his sermon. The churchwardens protested that he should be taken immediately to the doctor, but he would have none of it. He bade them and the agitated parishioners sit down, ordered the verger to bolt the doors and continued on the theme of Jeremiah for a further hour and twenty minutes.

Only after the blessing did the Rev'd Wenton suffer the doors to be opened and the doctor to be called. Even then he expressed regret that the sermon had been somewhat shorter than he had originally intended. Alas, by this time he had lost well nigh a gallon of blood and took to his bed, weak and fainting, never to rise from thence again. He died three days later on the eve of St Leonard's day. Had he not insisted on finishing his sermon, he would no doubt have made a complete recovery.

As for Sir Roderick, scarcely had the smoke from his pistol dispersed when he was overcome with remorse and revulsion at the enormity of his deed. He fled to the Lady Chapel, where he was still kneeling and weeping uncontrollably when the constable came to arrest him after the service. Refusing offers of bail, he went willingly to prison and was subsequently tried, convicted and sentenced to hang for murder. His last days were spent settling his debts and bequeathing what funds were left in charitable trusts for the relief of the poor young widows of the parish and their illegitimate offspring and for the comfort of abused horses.

Notwithstanding this last-minute change of heart, his name continued to be reviled, not least in the popular ballad "Sir Roderick Snebwood".

Many prayers were said by the good people of Smoatham for the repose of the soul of the Rev'd Isaiah Wenton and it was not until 1813 that any reason was found to suppose that their petitions may have been less than successful. At nine in the evening of November 5th the new verger, Henry Doghumble, was extinguishing the candles in St David's when he heard the sound of the doors being locked. Since he had the church keys about his person, he was surprised but not unduly alarmed. However, when he put any of the keys to its lock, 'twas to no avail; the door remained firmly shut. Then came a disembodied voice, beginning "May the words of my lips …" and continuing with a text from Jeremiah.

Now Henry was a devout man and not one to be afraid in the House of God even if he knew not whose voice it was that spake, so he dutifully sat down and listened. After an hour or so his concentration began to lapse, but still that spectral voice poured out in monotonous tones its trivial observations on the works of the prophet. At two minutes before five in the morning came the final "amen". Henry, dazed with boredom though he had been unable to sleep a wink, scarcely heard the locks creak open and was still sitting there when his anxious wife found him half an hour later.

Today, if you visit Smoatham, be sure to visit this beautiful church and admire the fine woodwork. If you look closely at the back of the pulpit you will see, at shoulder height, a blemish that has worn smooth over the years but is still unmistakably the mark of a bullet, and if you look very hard at the floor below, you may just make out an irregular patch that is stained darker than the rest. But if you go on the eve of St Leonard's day, be sure to leave before nine o'clock; unless, that is, you want to hear an eight hour discourse on the life and works of the prophet Jeremiah.

Bass Over Troubled Waters

The Beards Warden tunnel stands almost at the highest point of the Stiltford and Eyvesborough Canal where it climbs through the small hills between the North and South Drones. It is approached from the west via the Fletley locks - 25 of them. To the east there are two more locks before the canal begins its gradual descent into Dimley Vale.

Every year in Maytime several lay clerks from Stilchester Cathedral embark upon a weeks' trip around the Stiltshire Ring on the NB *Harmonia Ceoli*. On approaching the Beards Warden tunnel, any tenors on board are banished to their bunks while Mr Quainton Rhodes or one of his fellow basses will stand at the prow, don a sou'wester to ward off the drips and begin to sing.

The water is notoriously choppy - the course of the tunnel takes several twists and turns and there is a constant westward flow from the Lower Ryming reservoir into the locks - but the sound of a sonorous bass voice is known to sooth a boat's passage through the turbulent waters. Should a tenor so much as open his mouth, however, the boat will lurch into the tunnel walls with much scraping of paint and smashing of crockery, no matter how skilful the hand upon the tiller.

As you may have surmised, the tunnel is haunted. The restless spirit which agitates the water is that of Rosamund Gammon, a promising young contralto who was cruelly jilted by a tenor on the eve of their wedding.

Contrary to popular belief, the young lady did not commit suicide. She lived for more than six years after her betrayal, although she never sang again and spent much of the day quietly sobbing and wringing her hands. At the merest sound of a tenor voice she would be driven into a frenzy of weeping and wailing. The only person who could comfort her was the vicar of Beards Warden, a wise and kindly old man with a rich basso profundo voice.

And she was wont to walk the hills at night, wearing the bridal gown her aunt had made for the wedding that never was. One night in January 1853 she slipped and fell into the icy water near the eastern portal of the tunnel, whence she was swiftly swept by the treacherous current. Her lifeless body was found by the keeper at Fletley top lock the next morning.

The Bells of Scroterhouse

There are a number of tales concerning the mythical fourth college of the University of Stilchester but none as persistent as the belief that the bells of the long-gone (if it ever existed) college chapel will be heard when a fellow of the University is about to die "in harness".

This might be dismissed as mere fancy but for the well-attested fact that one of Stilchester's most distinguished academics, Dr Edwin Stywright, Master of St Cedd's, heard three bells tolling as he lay abed the night before his death in 1911. Again, this could be attributed to delirium arising from a terminal fever but for the testimony of his wife Gwendolyn who heard them as well and was prepared to swear as much on oath until her own death in 1927. Furthermore, Mrs Stywright was an accomplished musician, having been principal oboe of the Stilchester Philharmonic Orchestra for some 20 years and a piano teacher of note, and she recorded in her diary that the notes of the bells were "G (a little sharp), F and something short of E flat". This clearly rules out the three bells of All Souls without Sowgate, just 200 yards from the Stywrights' house, or indeed any feasible combination of three bells from any of the city churches or St Cedd's chapel.

The last time the ghostly bells were manifest was in 1989 when four Old College dons, taking port and brandy after a sumptuous and somewhat protracted dinner, claimed to have heard them around midnight. The following morning, Dr Owen Pencil, Professor of Classics at Old College, was found dead in his bed having suffered a stroke during the night.

The Damson Exchange

The Damson Exchange in Chineham Gregory is one of Stiltshire's finest secular buildings, comparable with the opulent Sievewrights' Hall in Stilchester, the Marquess of Eyvesborough's residence at Lower Crenton Place or that splendid monument to municipal pride, Eyvesborough Town Hall.

Built largely in the 16th century, it is a four-storey half-timbered building fronted by a sturdy stone tower which contains a magnificent turret clock and a clock chime of five smallish bells with fittings for occasional change ringing. The upper stories consist of a few offices, a large bar serving local ale and cider and sundry eating places. The ground floor is almost entirely open-plan with stout pillars supporting the floors above and large doors to permit the ingress of small vehicles.

It is here that, from June to October, local farmers set up their stalls to sell their produce to the wholesalers, caterers and jam makers – first strawberries, gooseberries and blackcurrants, then raspberries and redcurrants, later apples, plums and especially damsons. During the rest of the year the outstanding acoustics of this wonderful open space are put to good use when it becomes a venue for music and drama.

But there is one shameful episode in the building's history which has repercussions to this day. In 1708 a local woman, Maud Emmett, was accused by two farmers' wives of various misdemeanours including theft, sorcery and performing lewd acts with a black pig. On 25th September she was brought before the magistrates in the Damson Exchange, for in those days it also served as a courthouse. Despite obvious deficiencies in the prosecution case, not least the failure to locate the black pig, and the willingness of numerous people to testify to Maud's impeccable character, the magistrates ruled that she should be detained overnight in a locked cell in the building, pending further enquiries.

In the morning the poor woman was found to be dead and the stench of rotten fruit permeated the whole building. Not a single damson, plum or apple remained intact, let alone edible. In all, 33 cartloads of putrid vegetable matter were removed over the next two days and it was a good fortnight before the trading floor was pronounced fit for use. Even fruit in nearby houses had turned brown and mushy overnight. Such was the devastation at the height of the damson season that some families only escaped destitution thanks to public subscriptions from more fortunate neighbours.

The following year, on the exact anniversary, it happened again – every piece of fruit in the Exchange turned rotten - and again the next year, although this time most traders had taken the precaution of emptying their stalls the night before. In 1713 the Damson Counsel decreed that no trading should take place between the 25th and 27th of September, which decree has never been rescinded. Several exorcisms have been attempted over the years, but to no avail.

More than 300 years later the curse shows no sign of abating. The Exchange is still closed for three days in peak season, and a handful of fresh, firm damsons left on the floor overnight will be a pool of brown goo in the morning.

The Sorry Tale of the "Gostable Demon"

The coastal villages of Dongland boast some fine old inns, most of which can lay claim to be haunted, and one such is the Schooner in Gostable.

In the 1920s the Schooner employed a potman named Will Thumbwood. An unsociable character and none too bright, he was prone to getting drunk on the dregs from the pots and making lewd gestures and inappropriate remarks to young ladies. Indeed, such was his behaviour that the landlady eventual saw fit to fire him.

It was during the evening of 3rd September 1923, shortly after his dismissal, that one of the barmaids spotted him skulking around the back of the pub, probably up to no good, and bid him go away. But around 7.30 pm he burst into the bar, shaking with fear and shouting that he had seen a demon which reared up at him from behind an upturned boat, wailing horribly. Although it was dusk and he had been unable to see it clearly, he asserted that it was short of stature but "with a huge head like a wicker basket". The regulars simply laughed at him and about 20 minutes later he left. Shortly afterwards a group playing cribbage near the door heard a loud scream. "Sounds like Will's seen his demon again" said one and they chuckled and carried on with their game.

The first fishermen to set sail at dawn found Will Thumbwood's body in the harbour. It appeared that he had fallen backwards off the quay, hit his head on a mooring post and subsequently drowned.

Later that day, the mystery of the "demon" was solved. Young Peter Gland, the Sexton's son, had been pottering around the fishing boats when he somewhat unwisely thrust his head into the orifice of a lobster pot and was unable to withdraw it. As the fishermen had all gone home for the day and he was unable to see where he was going, he had blundered around for the next two or three hours, wailing pitifully, until his anxious father eventually found him. Once the lobster pot had been removed with the help of a little castor oil, Master Gland was none the worse for his ordeal, apart from having sore ears for the next few days.

But before long the spirit of Will Thumbwood began to haunt the Schooner and it still does to this day. Young ladies are particularly prone to the unwelcome attentions of the ghost. But should the supernatural harassment become unbearable, an upturned lobster pot placed on a pole behind the bar quickly restores the pub to its normal peace and tranquillity.

The Headless Butcher of Prokeworth

Many a town or village can boast a haunted inn or a haunted church but Prokeworth is possibly unique in having a haunted butcher's shop. To discover the reason for this unusual supernatural manifestation, we must go back to the sorry events which occurred in this quiet market town in the year 1815.

John Slope and James Fodder were life-long friends who entered the meat trade in their native Stilhaven and, having served their apprenticeships, moved to Prokeworth and set up in business together in a small shop next to the Black Boar Inn on the north side of the Square. Slope was a short, stocky man with a bushy moustache and somewhat volatile temperament but generally cheery and decidedly loquacious. Fodder, by contrast, had a rather gaunt appearance and more sanguine disposition. Both were more than usually fond of their ale.

It happened on the 23rd June that the news of Wellington's victory at Waterloo had just reached Stiltshire and the whole town was in festive mood. Around half past nine in the morning a footman from Prokeworth Manor called at the shop with an order for a large side of beef with which the household might celebrate the defeat of the French that evening. James Fodder went to the store room and selected a particularly fine carcase which he laid on the chopping block to prepare later before joining John Slope who had already adjourned next door for a quick celebratory quart or two.

Such is the way of these things that it was well after one o'clock when the two men staggered back to their shop, having suddenly realised that they had neglected their customers for some considerable time. Fodder, finding the task of opening the door more than sufficiently taxing for his befuddled brain, slid to the floor and fell asleep in the doorway. Slope, being marginally more compos mentis, stepped over him and glanced around for the queue of customers who might normally have been there at that time of day but then, seeing there were none, looked for a suitable place to take a nap. For reasons best known to himself, he chose to remove the carcase of beef from the slab and lie down in its place, covering himself with a sheet of muslin.

It was around four o'clock that Fodder awoke with a start, suddenly recalled the manorial order for the side of beef which the cook would have by now expected to have received and placed in the oven, shuddered at the mere thought of the consequences of offending the most prestigious customer in town and leapt up in a state of unmitigated panic. Seizing the largest cleaver from the rack, he rushed to the chopping block and seeing what he took to be the beef carcase in its muslin wrapping lying thereon, he set to work with a frenzy. After the first two or three strokes, it dawned upon him that something was not quite right. Fodder had jointed many a beef carcase in his thirty or so years, but never one that felt like this beneath his blade. He paused. Even as pushed aside the muslin, the blood began to ooze and then to spurt as the severed head of his colleague rolled slowly and then dropped off the end of the block.

With blood stained apron and cleaver still in hand, Fodder ran screaming from the shop and bumped into the kitchen boy who had been despatched by the irate cook to discover the whereabouts of the beef. The cleaver went flying into the crowd and fell upon a tinker, nicking his ear. As the sight of blood and blade and the sounds of shouting and screaming gradually filtered into fuddled brains, panic began to set in.

Within minutes there was such a commotion ensuing in the Square that the Constable was forced to rouse himself from his inglenook in the Bowl of Gruel to investigate. First, he was told by a florid fishwife that the Frogs were invading. Next, the tinker, squeaking in an animated falsetto that someone was trying to kill him, thrust the bloody cleaver into the Constable's hand. Eventually, he came across Fodder clinging to the market cross and sobbing hysterically and, deducing that something might be amiss in the Butchers' shop, made his way thither. Such was his shock upon seeing the grisly sight on the chopping block that he rushed straight into the Black Boar for something to steady his nerves and by all accounts could not be coaxed out until some time the following day.

James Fodder was put on trial for the murder of John Slope. Incriminating though the evidence was, so great was the number of witnesses prepared to testify to his impeccable character and to the cordial relationship between the two men, that the jury was eventually convinced that the incident must have been a ghastly accident and Fodder was acquitted. However, he never recovered from the ordeal and shortly afterwards was committed to a mental institution. After an unsuccessful attempt to sever his own head with a gardening implement, he was placed in a padded cell where he lived for a further fifteen years and died, a pathetic gibbering idiot.

During 1817, another butcher - a jovial chap called Herbert Ashenworth from Chineham Gregory - bought the shop but within months he was forced to leave, having been made bankrupt by lack of customers, and his 18 stone frame reduced to barely half that weight by strange and macabre goings on in the shop. Mysterious bloodstains would appear on cleavers, chopping blocks and pristine sheets of muslin. Carcases would be moved when no-one was looking or seem momentarily to take human form.

Numerous people claim to have seen the headless figure of John Slope searching for his former colleague, although whether 'tis to wreak his revenge or to pardon his friend for that dreadful deed no-one knows because of course no-one has ever seen the expression on his face.

Ilex Sanctus

Most English churchyards contain not a few trees, including that long-lived staple of folklore and legend, the yew. The holly is often present too but is at best a source of decoration for the yuletide festivities, at worst a giant weed, a wrecker of tombs and spoiler of vistas, to be ruthlessly pruned and rooted up.

Not so in Quisham, where the holly is revered on account of a strange tale, a local legend, or maybe it was only an old man's dream…

Many years ago, no-one knows when, a young maid of the parish died after being savaged by a bear escaped from a travelling circus. The poor girl, attempting to defend herself, had had one arm almost torn off and the other horribly gnawed by the beast.

On the day of the funeral, dark rain clouds lowered over Quisham. As the cortege reached the lych-gate, the heavens opened and most of the mourners sought shelter in the church until the worst of the storm had passed. The anxious sexton turned to the vicar and asked whether they should move the coffin into the safety of the church porch, but the priest indicated that it should remain where it was. Scarcely had the words left his lips when there was a tremendous clap of thunder and a mighty gust of wind swept the coffin from the trestles on which it rested and flung it into a nearby holly bush.

As the few bystanders approached with trepidation, the splintered wood began to quiver and the figure of the dead girl, her features pale as maggots by moonlight and clad in wisps of shrouding, rose slowly from the shattered coffin, whereupon the holly tree tenderly embraced her with its branches.

And as those good people watched in horrified fascination, the encircling branches underwent a strange metamorphosis, first taking on the appearance of bones which then, like those of Ezekiel's long-slain warriors, grew flesh and sinews until they resembled human limbs. The right arm attached itself seamlessly to the girl's shoulder. The left was plucked from the tree, whence it came away with a small sprig of leaves still attached, by a young man, one of the pall-bearers, who then held it against her side, and she smiled and thanked him as it took root.

Within hours, the young woman's colour had returned and she made a complete recovery, gaining full use of her new limbs. Soon afterwards she married the young man and they lived long and had many children, but only he ever saw the tiny sprig of holly leaves that grew from her left shoulder.

As for the tree, its descendants still flourish in Quisham churchyard where they are known as Ilex Sanctus or Holy Holly.

Knorrley Forest

In prehistoric times, the central lowlands of what is now Stiltshire were covered with a vast forest of native broad-leaved trees, predominantly oak and beech but also ash, elder, silver birch, hornbeam, rowan and hawthorn. From the Roman invasion to the Industrial Revolution, this great swathe of arboreal fecundity gradually receded and fragmented with the onslaught of civilisation, leaving only pockets of resistance. Of these, only three are of any great size. The most easterly, Bayconhurst Woods, is naturally lighter and sparser than the others. Oxbake Woods have been carefully managed as a source of timber for centuries.

Only Knorrley Forest, the largest and densest of these remnants, retains something of its primaeval splendour. Signs of human habitation are minimal and scattered around the periphery and few paths cross the middle which is thickly wooded to the point of impenetrability in places. Here, the eccentric 9th Duke of Stiltshire ran naked with the deer and allegedly talked to his extra-terrestrial mentor, Morfark. Here too, the notorious highwaymen of Spruntley Moor made their hideaway.

It is not a place for the faint hearted. No-one of sound mind ventures into Knorrley Forest after dark and few do so by day unless they know the area like the back of their hand, for many have gone that way and never returned. Tales have been told of giant foxes and fearsomely prodigious badgers, of gnarled trees that strangle the unwary traveller with their branches.

But the most intriguing denizens of the forest are the hog-goblins. Shy, reclusive creatures, they are seldom seen - elderly local inhabitants convinced of their existence will claim at most half a dozen sightings in a lifetime - but the descriptions are remarkably consistent. People who have seen one in profile or rear view as it scuttles for shelter describe it as looking like a wizened and bewhiskered old man, about four feet tall, clad in coarse, homespun garments with leather boots and waistcoat. [Curiously, it is always like an old man; the female of the species is either more adept at avoiding detection or looks exactly like the male.] Should a hog-goblin turn to look at you, its face momentarily assumes the features of a pig. And then it is gone, with the merest crackling of twigs as it blends into the undergrowth.

What are we to make of this? Sceptics will point to the presence of *amanita muscaria* and similar fungi in the woods and the propensity of the local people to eat wild mushrooms of any variety. The Rev'd Sidney Otter, the eminent naturalist, believed the hog-goblins to be humans who had acquired their distinctive characteristics through centuries of inbreeding and isolation from the rest of the world. But for most Stiltshire folk, hog-goblins are as Leprechauns are to the Irish; indeed, to see one's pig face is commonly regarded as an omen of extraordinary good fortune.

The Long Dafferd Cat

The village of Long Dafferd, some ten miles north-west of Stilchester, is banana shaped, moulded by the lower contours of Dafferd Downs and the western edge of Oxbake Woods. The road from Epfield to Cruftmere meanders through its centre and is called Lower Street; the only other thoroughfare runs more or less parallel but around ten to twelve feet higher and is known by the equally inspired name of Upper Street. The church of St Jerome stands above Upper Street, but many of the other buildings are set on sloping plots of land between the two roads, including three of Long Dafferd's four pubs: the Merperson, the Plough and the Giddy Goat all have two entrances, one on each level.

Thomson the cat belonged to old Mrs Blackaby at No. 43, Lower Street, but from the age of two or thereabouts spent most of his waking hours - and for that matter his sleeping ones - in the Plough Inn. This was not purely on account of the convivial surroundings, pleasant enough though they were, but due to an unslakeable thirst for ale. Now this is unusual in a cat. It is well known that horses love the stuff and not a few dogs enjoy a bowlful from time to time, but cats invariably turn up their noses at the slightest whiff of hops or the heady aroma of fermented malt. Not so Old Thomson. Ever since he knocked over Mrs Blackaby's glass of stout as a nine-week-old kitten, he had been addicted.

As soon as the Plough opened at eleven o'clock, he was there. Throughout the morning opening hours he would regularly lap the drip trays dry, take his customary libation from the regulars and pester visitors to follow suit. During the afternoon he would sleep in the churchyard or, in inclement weather, the church porch, returning to the Plough at six o'clock sharp for the evening session. If trade was slack, he would sometimes wander across to the Giddy Goat. After drinking-up time (when he was always on hand to assist anyone struggling to finish a pint) he could be seen rolling home, sometimes quite literally if he happened to leave the pub by the upper door.

But cat does not live by beer alone. Mrs Blackaby had long since given up feeding Thomson as his welfare became the shared responsibility of the village. When Ted the fishmonger popped into the Plough for his morning pint there was always something for Old Thomson in his pocket: the tail end of a cod or haddock, a few inches of fresh eel or, on Saturdays, his favourite - a plump, juicy bloater. In the evening there might be a plate of steak and kidney or liver and bacon to soak up the ale. At Sunday lunchtime there was always roast beef or shoulder of mutton to be had at the vicarage, with a piece of ripe Blefton Blue to round off the meal. It will not surprise you to learn that Old Thomson was a cat of impressive proportions. One or two people remember that he was once weighed and insist that he tipped the scales at three and a half stone.

He was never terribly enthusiastic about normal feline pursuits. Birds were of no interest to him; a sparrow might perch on his tail and he would do no more that flick it off with a gesture of mild annoyance. He sometimes caught the odd mouse in the cellar though no-one was quite sure how: opinion was divided as to whether he chose only the most infirm and slow-moving specimens, intimidated them with his sheer bulk or stunned them with alcohol fumes. As for balls of wool and suchlike: absolutely nothing would induce him to move a muscle unless it were edible or potable.

So far as anyone knows, Old Thomson left no progeny. He was, as they say, entire; but, whereas most village tom cats can boast scores of kittens in their likeness, Thomson seldom went courting even in his youth, being generally otherwise occupied. Occasionally he would leer drunkenly at a passing queen or make a half-hearted attempt at marking his territory with re-cycled best bitter. But it seems safe to surmise that he was for the most part totally incapable of discharging his duty towards the propagation of the species.

When he died in 1954 at the ripe old age of nineteen, his mortal remains were laid to rest in the bank of the churchyard overlooking the Plough. But his spirit continued to haunt the place. Drip trays and unattended glasses mysteriously emptied. Drinkers sitting on his favourite seats in the inglenook or the bench outside the lower door often became aware of his presence. Some would see out of the corner of an eye a large furry object sitting beside them but then, on turning to look closely, realise there was nothing there. Others might be conscious of a disembodied purr and the smell of beery breath. Dogs were puzzled, not knowing whether to bark and give chase or raise their hackles and growl; cats arched their backs and slunk away.

Then, in the 1960s, came the keg beer and the atmosphere in the Plough changed. Equipment continually malfunctioned; pipes would block, gas cylinders leak, taps hiss and belch. Older regulars would shake their heads and mutter darkly: "Tis Old Thomson's doing. 'Ee don't like it." "Aye, 'ee knew a good drop o' beer" "'Ee p****d better'n this stuff". But younger people came who didn't know and didn't care, life went on in Long Dafferd and ghostly goings-on faded into memories.

When the handpumps came back to the Plough, so did Old Thomson. Nowadays, Jim the landlord keeps a good cellar. He knows that, should the ale not be up to scratch, his most loyal regular would soon make his displeasure felt. But just to be on the safe side, whenever he taps a new cask, Jim always draws a big bowl and sets it on the floor and as soon as his back is turned it vanishes. Jim's steak and kidney pudding is justly popular with the customers and the portions are gargantuan, so nobody minds too much if a choice morsel disappears from the plate while they're not looking. Then there is the North Stilts branch of the Campaign for Real Ale: it must surely be the only one with a deceased feline for its President.

The Phantom of Ulm Water

Ulm Water is the largest inland body of water in Stiltshire: a roughly kidney-shaped lake about three miles long by one and a half wide, surrounded by flat, uninhabited countryside for several miles in any direction. There are two substantial islands and several tiny islets, but in other parts the water is deep and impenetrable. It can be a disquieting place even by day to a solitary walker or angler and positively eerie at night when the moon lies low and casts long shadows from the gnarled willows at the water's edge. But an atmosphere of utter foreboding hangs over the larger island.

Whatever it is that lurks there has been known about for centuries. In the library of St Cedd's College the Master's journal for 23rd October 1561 records that a student, one John Fylney, was "taken to ye physician, being delyrious and beside hymself with fear, having seen ye phantom of Ulme Water". In 1728 the Parish Clerk of Ulm St Mary wrote that two men from Oxbake had been rescued from the island one morning after their terrified screams were heard by a farmer on the shore. It appears that they had been ambushed, rowed there and abandoned by a gang from Jupton the previous evening but were unable to articulate exactly what had happened during the night. One showed no physical symptoms and in due course recovered from his ordeal but the other began to foam at the mouth, succumbed to a fever that evening and died two days later.

However, these seem to have been isolated incidents. By and large, local people shunned the area after dark and visitors seldom came that way. Doubtless there were other manifestations of the phantom prior to the late nineteenth century but they have not been recorded.

The most celebrated case concerning Ulm Water occurred in 1895. Three years earlier a wealthy businessman by the name of Robert Worley, not a native of Stiltshire, had moved into the area with his wife and three children and built a handsome house in beautiful gardens about half a mile from the lake's southern shore. This pleasant homestead was called *Tippledown* - an innocent enough name but one that was later seen to show a dreadful prescience - and during the summer it was used to entertain a succession of house guests including some old friends, the Crisp family.

In the afternoon of August 17th, the Worley children, Edwin (aged 11), Sophia (9) and Victoria (5), together with the Crisp's son, James (8), set out to explore the lake in a rowing boat. When they failed to return by nightfall, the alarm was raised and the local policeman with a posse of volunteers from the village began a systematic search of the area. Many of these good men had severe misgivings about setting foot on the large island (strangely, it has never been given a name), but the knowledge that young lives were at risk drove them to overcome their fears and make a hasty but thorough examination of the place. When it was announced that Mr Worley had offered a substantial reward they redoubled their efforts, but it was all to no avail: no sign of children or boat was found that night.

The search resumed at dawn and it was not long before the boat was spotted drifting at the northern end of the lake with little Victoria lying asleep in the bows. The child was unable to explain what had happened; indeed, within a matter of days she seemed to have erased the incident from her memory entirely. Meanwhile, the party which returned to the large island found the lifeless body of Edwin lying face down at the water's edge. There was no sign of injury but his right hand grasped a stick as though he had been trying to defend himself or his companions. Both islands were searched many times and the lake scoured with drag nets but the bodies of Sophia and James were never recovered, although large numbers of ancient and unidentified bones were brought to the surface. Not surprisingly, the Worleys left the area shortly afterwards and *Tippledown* - or "triple drown" as it quickly became known - fell into disrepair. The ruin still stands, adding another eerie touch to that bleak landscape.

In 1920, at the Dipsomaniacs' Club in Eyvesborough, Ezra Nallory and George Swist accepted a wager from the actor Sebastian Thrice-Wessley who promised them 100 guineas apiece if they would spend a night on the large island. On 15th October, just before sunset, they rowed out to the island, taking with them a small tent, hurricane lamps, provisions and a bottle of extremely good cognac put up by Thrice-Wessley as part of the deal. He, with two of his gamekeepers, patrolled the shores of the lake to ensure that the bargain was kept. The evening passed uneventfully until eleven o'clock. Nallory's diary records what happened next:

"Not long finished supper when the lamps went out. Tried to re-light them and failed. It was as if a wind blew from within the lamp itself. Odd. Took some brandy and turned in. Tried to sleep. Now about midnight. Lamps still won't light, so writing by moonlight. God, this is a frightful place. Need a good shot of cognac."

"1 a.m. Getting cloudy - can't see to write. Cognac nearly finished. Feel a bit drowsy now."

The next few entries were scrawled in a shaky hand a few hours later:

"Must have slept a bit and was awakened by Swist getting up to relieve himself. Looked at my pocket watch and it was about 2.30. Took some more brandy. Swist seemed to have been gone a long time but I was too weary to go after him. Felt as if something was trying to draw a veil over my senses."

"Woke at ten to seven. Almost light. Swist's sleeping bag empty. Forced myself to get up despite still feeling half paralysed. Called to Swist. No sign of him near tent."

"Found him - Lord, I feel sick, but I must write [Nallory, it should be noted, was a scientist and retained the presence of mind to record the events in scrupulous detail] - at the other end of the island. Lying face down. Cold. Eyes glazed. Right hand grasping rock. Looks dishevelled but no injuries. No marks on ground. The air is oppressive, I'm going to choke. Can't stay here."

At 7.30 Nallory, having rowed ashore, made contact with the gamekeepers. They had seen or heard nothing untoward. The post mortem on Swist gave the probable cause of death as heart failure.

One afternoon in 1936, Jean-Pierre DuBois, a Frenchman on holiday, took it into his head to swim across Ulm Water. It seems that the undertaking proved more strenuous than he had supposed, so he stopped to rest on the island, fell asleep and did not wake before nightfall. The following morning, he swam back and arrived at a farmhouse on the outskirts of Smitley, wide-eyed, exhausted and panic stricken. He was taken to the Lonchelsea Sanatorium, where he slept for 36 hours.

His behaviour on awakening was bizarre to say the least: at times he would mumble "les six" and roll his eyes horribly in between uttering the most appalling shrieks and groans. [The registrar, a man well versed in contemporary music, opined that he must be voicing his disapproval at the works of Honegger, Milhaud et al, but the nurses were not convinced by this theory.] Then he would murmur "Angelique", close his eyes and drift into a peaceful sleep. In due course, Mme DuBois arrived from Lyon and proved not to be called Angelique nor, to her knowledge, did her husband have a mistress of that name. Eventually he made a full recovery and returned home, contributing nothing further by way of explanation of his ordeal.

During the Second World War, a badly damaged bomber returning from Germany limped over the Stiltshire coast with engines blazing and crash landed on the South Drones. Hopes that the crew had managed to bail out were justified when the tail gunner walked into Smitley Police Station early in the morning. He confirmed that all four had parachuted. He said he had landed in water and swum twenty yards or so to shore and believed his comrades to have come down some distance away "in the middle of the lake or possibly on an island". Fearing the worst, the Sergeant despatched his men to Ulm Water.

Of the other three crew members only the co-pilot, Lt. Francis Oatman, was found alive. He insisted that both the pilot and the fore-gunner had also landed safely but that during the night they had lost contact while trying to determine their whereabouts. Eventually, overcome with drowsiness, he had lain down and slept. At dawn, he soon realised that he was on an island and set off to find the others. The gunner was lying on the shingle, much as George Swist had lain. Before long the police launch arrived, having already recovered the pilot's body from the water.

John Finley grew up in Ulm St Mary during the 1960s. A taciturn, studious boy who preferred his own company and that of Mother Nature to playing with other children, he developed a fascination with the Water and the stories surrounding it, which became all the keener when he heard of his near-namesake and the first recorded sighting of the phantom four centuries earlier. While a student at St Cedd's, he made the acquaintance of Professor Simeon Thrule, an acknowledged expert on the history and folklore of Stiltshire.

After he left university, Finley's fascination with Ulm Water started to take the form of a dangerous obsession. He began to talk of spending a night on the island. A friend, Peter Foggert, a young man of immense bravado and arguably little sense, rashly offered after a few drinks to accompany him. But Finley hesitated to accept the offer. He mulled the available data over in his mind: Fylney, presumed alone - delirious but survived. Two Oxbake men - one died, one survived. The Worley children - one dead, two missing, presumed drowned, one survived. Nallory and Swist - one died, one survived. DuBois - alone and survived. Three airmen - one drowned, one dead on land, one survived. One survived! Slowly the inexorable conclusion dawned on Finley: if he wanted to see the phantom and live to tell the tale, he would have to go alone.

Meanwhile, Professor Thrule, examining some manuscript fragments from the Eyvesborough assizes of the 14th century, came across a fascinating discovery. In 1392, seven sisters named Errent from the Parish of Ulm St Mary had been accused of witchcraft and subjected to ordeal by water. The youngest, Ruth, a girl just thirteen years of age, had drowned and was thus deemed innocent. Unusually, the clerk recorded that she was a fair child with golden hair and that she was buried in St Mary's churchyard. The other six were sentenced to death by burning but then drowned for the sake of practicality; the manuscript does not state where, but there is only one sizeable body of water in that part of the county. Although some of the charges were predictably fanciful, there seems to have been strong evidence linking the older sisters with several murders, robberies and other heinous crimes.

As he penned an excited letter to his young protégé, the professor was struck by an intriguing thought. Suddenly the Frenchman's ramblings about "les six" and "Angelique" began to make sense. He thought about little Victoria Worley, made a discrete phone call to a senior RAF officer of his acquaintance and the following day received confirmation from the archives that Lt Oatman had indeed been the youngest member of the ill-fated bomber crew. He already knew that Nallory, at 33, had been two years younger than Swist. Immediately he phoned John Finley, but there was no reply.

Unknown to the professor, Finley had chosen that very evening to make his trip to the island. Peter Foggert ferried him across in his father's motor boat and left him there with a bivouac, a sleeping bag, a thermos flask and a pile of sandwiches. Several hours - and pints - later, Foggert began to have reservations about leaving his friend on the island and just before midnight, notwithstanding Finley's insistence on being alone, he returned to the boat moored at the lakeside, started the outboard motor and set out across the still water towards the foreboding black shape that lay ahead.

He had cut the throttle to coast the last few yards when he saw Finley, who had heard the roar of the outboard, shouting and waving at him frantically to turn around. They are both able to describe what happened next. At first it was just a faint glimmer on the surface, then six eerie blue lights seemed to rise from the water and move towards the island, spreading out as if to encircle the two men. Foggert had by this time scrambled out of the boat and the two stood transfixed as the six shapes advanced. They knew that total silence prevailed and yet in their heads both experienced the most blood-curdling groaning and wailing.

Then, their attention was drawn to the horizon where a speck of bright white appeared. Briefly its glow picked up the silhouette of St Mary's spire like a faint floodlight and then it moved rapidly towards them, growing larger as it flitted across the water. Again they became aware of the blue spectres now closing in on them, their willowy forms at once sinister and strangely sensual like exotic dancers. Each man felt these awful beings were intent upon him alone, while the hideous music in his head reached a crescendo with a harmony of bowel-chilling intensity that no composer of horror film soundtracks could emulate in a million years.

But still that blob of light sped over the dark waters until it too was upon them, brilliant white and gold, subtle and sensuous but beautiful beyond description. For what might have been a split second or half of eternity it seemed that some dreadful Manichean struggle ensued, and then the torturous music faded, the blue spectres retreated, twitching angrily as though thwarted of their prey, and the pure bright one blossomed with such radiance that her evil siblings melted away into the lake as she engulfed their would-be victims.

Both Finley's and Foggert's memories of the incident stop there. Finley awoke first, shortly after dawn, and roused his friend. Of the boat there was no sign. Fortunately, Foggert's father had raised the alarm when his son failed to return with the boat. A few fragments of the vessel were later found drifting ashore, looking for all the world as though the tiny craft had been blown up by a substantial charge of high explosives. But the two men were recovered and, apart from suffering mild shock, none the worst for their ordeal.

Professor Thrule arrived shortly, having driven down from Strupton after repeatedly failing to contact Finley by phone. In the light of his findings, the descriptions of the night's proceeding certainly made some kind of sense. But Finley was puzzled: why were they both alive to tell the tale? The professor was even more puzzled: had "Angelique" excelled herself this time?

John Finley's parents had left Ulm St Mary some years earlier. That afternoon, Peter Foggert's mother telephoned them to tell them the story. Mrs Foggert knew Mrs Finley quite well; after all, some 23 years earlier they had both been in Grencham Cottage Hospital and spent several hours in the labour ward together....

Shortly after this, the Bishop of Stilchester conducted an exorcism the like of which has never been seen before or since. Finley and Professor Thrule had located young Ruth's long-lost grave and prayers were said for the repose of her poor innocent soul, but not before the entire shoreline of the lake and the island had been thoroughly purged with bell, book and candle.

That was more than twenty years ago and no-one has died or seen strange apparitions there since. But Ulm Water is still an eerie, lonely and disquieting place, the island as dark and foreboding as ever. Could there be some primaeval force of evil which drove the Errent sisters to their errant ways and makes simple god-fearing people instinctively stay away?

Tram 19

Most of the rolling stock on Stilchester's tramways dates from its inception in 1922 or soon after, although there have been numerous refurbishments and technical upgrades over the years. To say the trams have character would be an understatement; they all have unique personalities although, curiously, they are always referred to by number rather than name. Drivers tend to have a career-long relationship with one particular tram, although the trams change routes on a regular basis. There were originally three routes: 1 "North", 2 "Academical" (so called because it passes all the UoS colleges and the Academy) and 3 "South". Route 4 "Outer" was not instituted until 1970.

The 30th November 1962 seemed a fairly ordinary day – rather dull and overcast, some light drizzle and blustery wind – when Fred Grubber reported for his early shift at 6 am. He climbed into the cab of Tram 19, turned the key and grasped the dead man's handle – and nothing happened. He removed the key, replaced it, murmured "Come on old girl" and tried again. The tram wouldn't budge. The power must be on, he reasoned, because number 4 was just leaving the depot on Route 1 but 19's voltmeter showed zero.

After a few more tries to no avail, Fred went to find the Depot Foreman, who scratched his head and said "OK, I'll get the engineer onto it. Meanwhile you'd better take number 22". Reluctantly Fred took the spare keys for number 22 and got into the cab. Like 19, it wouldn't respond. His colleagues Bert and Archie were having similar problems with 20 and 21. Soon it became apparent that all six trams on Route 3 weren't going anywhere.

As all the trams on Routes 1 and 2 had already left the depot, apart from 5 and 12 which were undergoing maintenance, there was nothing they could do but wait. After about 20 minutes crawling around under the trams, Ted the duty engineer emerged, shaking his head. He had to admit that he was just as baffled as the drivers and could do no more until the maintenance crew arrived and they could conduct a more thorough investigation.

It was just before 7 o'clock when the phone on the Foreman's desk rang. The local police sergeant had called to say that a large oak tree had fallen across the tramlines between St Jude's and St Raphael's Hospital. With typical police precision he confirmed that the incident had taken place at 6.34 and had been witnessed by three people. Fortunately, no-one was injured. Fred, who was in the office, was not slow to grasp the import of this. Had Number 19 left the depot at the scheduled time, they would have been right there at that very moment!

Just then the General Manager arrived and had to be appraised of the situation. The crews on Routes 1 and 2 were beginning to return from their first circuit and wanted to know what was going on. And a reporter from the Stilchester Gazette had somehow heard the news already and was looking for an interview. Amid the ensuing hubbub, Fred quietly slipped away and returned to Number 19.

He sat in the cab and whispered softly "You knew, didn't you?". The needle of the voltmeter flickered. Fred turned the key and put his hand on the dead man's handle. The motor purred as he drove the tram forward a few yards and then back again. He removed the key and patted the dashboard. "Well done, old girl! I reckon you deserve a day off."

The Ruckworth Pepper

To the west of the village of Ruckworth is a small, fertile valley, carved out by a long-vanished tributary of the Stilt. Its steep banks are covered with gnarled trees and dense, almost impenetrable scrub. From the old river-bed, hot springs bubble to the surface, creating a peculiarly warm and humid climate within that sheltered environment. It is said that within this valley grows a plant, the fruit of which is so hot that should anyone eat it their mouth will burn for a year and a day.

Legend has it that many centuries ago the Devil came for the soul of the Rector*, a man infamous for gambling and debauchery and commonly believed to be a practitioner of the black arts and responsible for the disappearance of several young children. As the Devil knocked on the front door of the Rectory, the evil cleric made his escape through the kitchen window and fled the village with the horned one in hot pursuit. In some versions of the tale, the Devil climbed the church steeple, the better to see his quarry, which is why to this very day the weathercock wears a startled expression on his face. It was in the little valley that the Devil caught up with the Rector and carted him off to the underworld, leaving behind the strange plant as a memento of his visit.

Although few people claim to have seen the Ruckworth Pepper within living memory, belief in its existence is strong. Mothers still threaten misbehaving children with it (cf. the Epficld Hump). Botanists agree that a plant of the capsicum family could indeed survive in the almost sub-tropical conditions of the Ruckworth Valley and have even suggested that it may have been planted there, whether deliberately or inadvertently, by the Rev'd Sydney Otter who is known to have bred such exotica in his greenhouses at Thrimp Rectory. However, the legend predates Otter by at least two centuries.

The Stiltshire recording studio Ruckworth Pepper Records is named after this enigmatic plant.

* Believed to be Cuthbert de Brabazon (Rector from 1398-1414) who is mentioned in the chapter records at Stilchester Cathedral as being suspected of heresy and whose incumbency was followed by a lengthy interregnum, presumably because no respectable clergyman was prepared to take on a living so tainted with the forces of darkness.

The Verger's Tunnel

Behind the Observatory in Stilchester, a narrow, U-shaped ramp slopes down some thirty feet to a small but ornate portal and on the opposite bank, close to the Market, is a similar one. These are the two entrances to a foot tunnel beneath the Stilt, built in 1838-40 to the design of Bishop Matthew Grisel, an amateur civil engineer of some note. It is a narrow, brick-lined structure, no more than a yard and a half at its widest and barely six feet high. The lighting is dim and occasional ferns grow upon the damp walls.

The frequent puddles of water on the floor need cause the subterranean pedestrian no alarm; in 1912 the City Council, observing the tendency of some uncouth persons to use the tunnel mouths as a convenience, installed at each end an ingenious clockwork device which flushes the walkway at half-hourly intervals with several gallons of water syphoned from the river whilst using the water pressure to rewind its motor. These machines were built by the inventor, Horace Burnthrope and are the only examples of his work still in operation.

In September 1839, when construction was well under way, with the boring completed but the lining still in progress, certain unseemly goings-on were reported at the Cathedral. The Canon Almoner, noting a shortfall in the offertory, voiced his concerns to the Dean who instigated an immediate and thorough investigation. The finger of suspicion began to point to Sidney Flount, aged 33, a Verger who had been in the Cathedral's employ for about two years.

As evidence mounted, the trap was laid: towards the end of Evensong, the Dean, the Almoner and a member of the City Constabulary concealed themselves in the robe cupboard adjoining the Vergers' vestry. In due course, Flount entered bearing the collection plate and was seen trousering a handful of coins. At this the two clerics and the officer of the law leaped out to apprehend the miscreant but Flount, being a wiry and athletic fellow, managed to evade the Constable's grasp and fled into the cloisters. The three gave chase in the twilight but lost sight of him behind the Bishop and Sunset.

It appears that Flount had gone straight to the tunnel, hoping thereby to make his escape through the narrow, crowded streets of the east bank. In the dark he ran headlong into the end of a scaffold pole which struck him in the eye with such force as to fracture his skull in three places. The coroner opined that he must have lain unconscious for several hours while slowly bleeding to death. His body was discovered by the workmen early the next morning.

Within weeks of the tunnel's opening, rumours that it was haunted began to circulate and before long it became known as the Verger's Tunnel (hardly surprisingly, as the official name of the Sub-Stilt Promenade failed to fire the public imagination). To be sure it is a spooky place after dark, but the curious thing is that nobody has ever claimed to have seen or heard Sidney Flount's ghost; people just assume it ought to be there.

The Witches of Wizards Alton

Like most English counties, Stiltshire has had its fair share of witches, wise women, warlocks and various persons of pagan interests. Stiltshire folk over the centuries have been generally tolerant of such people, believing them to be at best purveyors of an ancient craft of healing and miracle working, and at worst harmless eccentrics. In the days of the witch hunts the county came under scrutiny and at first roused the interest of the witchfinders. In many a tavern could be found people who, on being plied with a few quarts or slipped the odd shilling, could be relied upon to recount lurid tales of child sacrifice, of flying broomsticks, or of elderly women indulging in unnatural practices with black cats or, more usually (this being Stiltshire), black pigs. However, on closer examination, the alleged perpetrators of these acts invariably proved to be strangers whom no-one could identify, victims' names were curiously absent from parish registers and the secret glade in the middle of the forest always turned out to be one of a dozen such clearings, each with a blasted elm or a prominent ring of mushrooms. In the end the inquisitors, faced with this lack of hard evidence, even by their standards, and increasingly out of pocket, turned their attention to other regions where the locals were more willing to betray their neighbours for the price of a pint or two.

But there is one village in Stiltshire which has had more than its fair share of association with the supernatural. Originally called Alton, it was home in the thirteenth century to a magician, by all accounts a powerful and charismatic character who built up a following of mostly female devotees. Little else is known of him now but such was his fame at the time that the name of the village acquired the prefix "Wizards" which remains to this day.

There is one curious artefact in the vicinity – an ancient menhir which might be just like any other standing stone but for a large replica of a human nose which protrudes from one side. Whether it was sculpted from a natural protuberance in the rock or by painstakingly chipping away at a much larger block of stone, the nose is extremely life-like, even down to the hairs which, although somewhat eroded over the centuries, are still visible in the nostrils.

Whether because of some inherent mystic quality of the place (some say it is a confluence of ley lines) or simply because of its name, Wizards Alton has attracted persons of paranormal leanings over the years. The most notable instance was in the 1920s, when a short, stocky man with flowing black hair calling himself Hermes Brunato purchased a large derelict house called Hemlock Hall and set up a community consisting of himself and a group of dark haired, pale skinned young women. He became known locally as The Wizard, an appellation of which he seemed thoroughly to approve.

The inhabitants of Hemlock Hall tended to keep themselves to themselves, although the women were occasionally seen gathering herbs from the hedgerows or buying provisions in the village shop, where they were generally shunned or regarded with suspicion by the good wives of the neighbourhood. But on moonlit nights they were known to gather within a circle of trees on the edge of the village close to the ancient lichen-clad monolith, where they danced naked and with great abandon for the gratification of their master or, during his not infrequent absences, for their own amusement. Mr Quainton Rhodes recalls the story told to him by his Uncle Teddy who, as a young lad of 15, went to watch the witches dance. He hid behind a bush and gazed wide-eyed, transfixed by the swirling black tresses, the heaving bosoms and pale, plump buttocks gleaming in the moonlight - until one of the witches turned and slowly winked at him, whereupon he fled red-faced, jumped on his bicycle and pedalled furiously all the way home to Aggerby.

The community flourished for about three years before its activities came to an abrupt end. For the story of the day of reckoning we turn to the testimony of Sidney Blagness, a carter by trade. On 14th June 1928 he was taking his lunch in the station yard at Kings Pebberworth, having just unloaded a consignment of bales of cloth, when he was approached by a large, stony-faced woman who enquired whether he could drive her to Wizards Alton. He agreed and drove briskly, whistling in his accustomed manner while his passenger sat unsmiling and tight lipped beside him. Once in the village, she asked him to take her to Hemlock Hall and to wait while she attended to some business.

Almost as soon as she entered the house, there were sounds of great vituperation from within. Minutes later she emerged, dragging the Wizard by his ear and subjecting him to a non-stop torrent of verbal abuse. Between the front door and the gate she had denounced him for abandoning his family, consorting with trollops, provoking the wrath of the Almighty by practising alchemy and wearing a ridiculous wig. Whilst climbing onto the cart she had further accused him of flirting with Satan, bringing disgrace upon his former regiment and neglecting his dahlias. In the absence of any instruction, Blagness turned his horses towards Kings Pebberworth and listened in amazement as this formidable woman continued her tirade, without apparently pausing for breath, for the entire hour and a quarter's duration of the journey.

The facts as Blagness gleaned them are these. The Wizard's real name was Herbert Brown, he was an actuary and lived in a semi-detached house in a respectable suburb of Birmingham. Mrs Brown, for it was she, had become suspicious of his frequent absence on "business trips" and, acting on two clues, a fragment of the Stiltshire Gazette found in his jacket pocket and a dusty grimoire hidden in the attic, had made enquiries and eventually determined his true whereabouts.

On arrival at the station, she thrust half a crown into Blagness' palm while telling her husband how the cat had been suffering an unduly severe attack of fleas which was obviously demonically induced as a direct result of evil goings-on in Wizards Alton. As the carter climbed back into his seat and took up the reins, he could still hear her voice blaming the miserable Herbert for causing her aged mother's rheumatism. Subsequently, on relating the tale to his brother, a porter at Stilchester Central, he learned that the monologue was still in full spate when the pair changed trains an hour later. The experience had a profound effect on Sidney Blagness and he went to his grave some thirty years later believing his own wife, who was not exactly blunt of tongue, to be a model of virtue and restraint.

Herbert Brown was never seen in Wizards Alton again. Of his coven, one or two drifted away soon afterwards. The remainder stayed at Hemlock Hall and opened a tea shop, which became very popular with the tourists. Local people were more wary; "Won't catch me drinking that witches' brew!" they would say.

Miscellaneous Hauntings

In addition to the spooky and often bizarre phenomena chronicled in these pages, Stiltshire is home to many more ghostly goings-on, a few of which we will mention briefly here.

The Lovers' Leap

The Vicarage at St Togan is reputedly haunted by the ghosts of a former Vicar and his daughter. The poor girl and her lover leapt from the high cliffs above which the village stands after being refused permission to marry by her father. Shortly after this tragic incident the Vicar fled the village, having been denounced as cruel and unreasonable by his wife, the Bishop, the Archdeacon and the vast majority of his parishioners. He died, a lonely and broken man, in a garret in Brinceton less than a year later and his restless spirit still returns to crave the forgiveness of his daughter, which is never granted.

The Fiddler o' Fudwell

Night-time travellers on the long and lonely road which leads past Fudwell churchyard towards Pittlebore have sometimes heard what sounds like a lone fiddler playing an eerie and haunting melody. This is not, as you might suppose, an omen of death or misfortune; on the contrary it often seems to presage a birth, a wedding or an unexpected windfall.

The Joyless Sailor

The pubs in St Enoch's are haunted by a ghost known as the Joyless Sailor, who moves freely between the Mermaid, the Lobster and the Enoch's Head. The miserable mariner is believed to be searching for his long-lost sweetheart who was one of the Maids of St Enoch. Although sightings have been noted for at least 200 years the ghost has recently been spotted in the Yacht which only opened in 2011.

The Phantom Plough

Growell is where the annual Stiltshire Ploughing Championships are held. Occasionally a phantom plough, without horses or tractor, is seen to glide through the village at midnight on the eve of the contest, leaving deep ruts across the village green and the churchyard. This does not bode well for the local team's chances of success. It also betokens an enormous amount of mouldy bread and cheese in the village over the next few days.

Needless to say, Stiltshire has more than its fair share of porcine phantoms:

The Black Pig of Clamburton

A fearsome-looking, hairy black pig is sometimes seen running through the trees on the edge of the village, close to the churchyard. Some say it is the ghost of the Ninth Duke of Stiltshire whose ancestral home Clamburton Hall stood nearby.

The Gristlecombe Boar

An even more fearsome beast, perhaps more like a wild boar than a domestic pig, this one has been seen only a handful of times in the past five centuries. But its blazing red eyes, blood-curdling roar and propensity to turn beer sour and frighten children and dogs (sometimes allegedly to death) have ensured it a place in local folklore.

The Sow and Piglets

Anyone walking near the low, muddy banks of the Stilt just north of Smoatham on the night of 24th January might expect to hear frantic squealing or even glimpse a ghostly sow and her litter. Their fleshly counterparts were drowned when their sty slid into the river during a ferocious storm on this day in 1858.

The White Pig of Aggerby

Aggerby is in the heart of pig rearing country, indeed one of the local breeds is known as "Pride of Aggerby", but this particular phantom porker has been likened to the now extinct "Stiltshire White" which was abandoned more than a century ago for being too lean. A most benign spectre, it is only ever seen in the church - entering through the west door (whether open or closed), trotting past the font and up the aisle or standing on its hind legs at the lectern as if to read a lesson.

And finally...

Obervole

Obervole, on the edge of Knorrley Forest, has the dubious distinction of being the most haunted place in Stiltshire. St Jude's church, the Rugged Oak Inn and many of the older houses are constructed almost entirely of wood from the forest, which many claim is the reason they are so conducive to paranormal activity. Ghosts include three weeping widows, a naked curate (though he still wears his dog collar), a one-armed postman, a luminous badger, a little girl with a skipping rope but no feet and a demented dentist of fairly recent origin.

Seasonal Stiltshire

The county still resonates to the rhythms of the changing seasons and the liturgical calendar.

Christmas in Stiltshire

Christmas in Stiltshire has changed little over the centuries. Stiltshire folk, being by and large God-fearing people and still attuned to the natural rhythms of life, tend not to be drawn into the pre-Christmas orgy of spending and partying but wait patiently for the season of Advent to take its course. Seldom is a lighted tree seen in a living room window before Christmas Eve (except perhaps in Lonchelsea). But then, without six weeks of anticipation to dull the appetite, the celebration begins in earnest. For the next 12 days hardly anyone goes to work except publicans and clergy people. Grocers, butchers and bakers open their doors for the odd hour or two to provide the basic necessities of life.

As always, a Stiltshireman's belly is never far from his mind. The typical family, after attending Matins and maybe taking a brisk stroll along the frost-clad lanes with perhaps a brief stop for a quart of old ale at some convivial inn, will go home, put the oven on and later sit down to a lengthy five or six course meal, the centrepiece of which will be a plump roast goose. (The ubiquitous turkey never supplanted the goose as it has everywhere else in Britain, although the Breen Brown turkey, a semi-wild breed descended from a few birds which escaped from a farm in the 1950s has been seen on trendier tables in recent years.) This is often accompanied by a fine claret or burgundy, although rural families following the peasant tradition may have lovingly nurtured a small cask of farmhouse cider from the vintage of two or three years ago, and followed with a rich home-made Christmas pudding with brandy butter or rum sauce and then cheese, either a well matured Blefton Blue or, in the North Drones, a slice of piquant local Repstock with a mince pie.

In Dongland, shellfish feature prominently on the menu. The fishermen of Japhetstowe put to sea on Christmas Eve to check their lobster pots and the famous crab market opens for business on Christmas morning - but not before the Rector has celebrated Holy Communion on the quay. This is a joyous family service and the largest crabs of the night's catch are taken up in the offertory procession by the fishermen's children. Then, as the ten bells of St Thomas ring out in the frosty air, the quayside pubs open their doors and the fish stalls start trading. Almost every family goes home with a handsome crustacean with which to start their Christmas dinner, or else they enjoy a crab sandwich and a pint of black velvet on the quay.

Local yuletide customs abound. In the North Drones there is a great tradition of carol singing on Christmas Eve (when else?) and some villages have their own unique carols such as the Flockshaw Wassail or the Song of the Repstock Waits. The singers are sometimes accompanied by fiddle, melodeon or hurdy-gurdy and always the bassoon. In Hogberrow, on Boxing Day, the bell ringers roast pigs on the Glebe and the crispy ears are nailed to an ancient yew tree where they are supposed variously to detect imprecisions in the ringers' striking or record items of salacious gossip in the village.

New Year's Eve is the occasion for much ringing of bells. In most places, due no doubt to the impracticality and possible danger of hurriedly removing muffles from the clappers, ringing before and after midnight is not done; the custom at the Cathedral and many parish churches is to ring the old year out and drink the new one in, although in some rural parts the reverse procedure is followed with somewhat cacophonous results.

Then comes Twelfth Night and an end to the festivities. At Urnstone, to herald the dawn of Epiphany, the young men go around the houses, across the fields and through the woods carrying a turnip lantern atop an absurdly long pole, symbolising the Star of Bethlehem, while some of their elders dress up in oriental finery and others as pantomime camels to re-enact the journey of the Magi. (Any number of Wise Men may take part, since nowhere in the Bible is it stipulated that there were three of them.) Meanwhile, the women very sensibly stay indoors with a few bottles of something heart-warming which they have invariably finished - or least pretend as much - by the time their menfolk return.

Goose has been eaten in Stiltshire on Christmas Day since time immemorial. Particularly prized is the goose which has been "blessed" by a robin. This event is somewhat of a rarity on account of the fact that the timid and frail robin is seldom found in close proximity to the somewhat larger and more robust fowl. Nevertheless the tradition persists, based on one of the more obscure (and possibly misquoted) utterances of the Blessed Witta: "When robin trampleth on foot of goose, then shall man and pig rejoice". Indeed, it was not unknown for children to be assigned the task of bringing about this unlikely juxtaposition of avian species before the geese were slaughtered on the last Monday in Advent.

The accompaniments to the goose are many and varied – spiced cherries and red onions, wild mushrooms and cider brandy, pureed parsnips and fried leeks - except in the village of Urnstone where it is usually eaten with mashed potatoes. This custom originated in the early 1800s when an ascetic sect called the Beezleyites (after their founder, Obadiah Beezley who was believed to be a reincarnation of John the Baptist) flourished in the area. The Beezleyites subsisted almost entirely on mashed potatoes and, while some of the more moderate members were able to countenance the eating of goose once a year, roasting potatoes in the goose fat was considered an indulgence too far. The sect disbanded after Obadiah's death in 1869 but the Beezleyite rallying cry of "we has mash" reverberates in the souls of their descendants who still inhabit the area.

The Flockshaw Wassail

Wassail! Wassail! Wassail! Wassail! Wassail!

The sheep within the fold do lie,
The hogs are in the pound,
While we do trudge through wind and
snow
To sing this joyful round.

So hearken then ye villagers
And list to what we do say,
That Christ the Saviour of the world
Was born upon this day.

As to your fireside ye go
To flee the biting air,
Remember Jesus came to earth
In stable grim and bare.

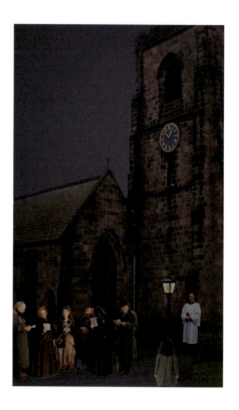

We see ye have your parlour decked
With branches green and young,
In memory of the Lamb of God
Who on the tree was hung.

We trust ye've brewed a goodly cask
Of strong and wholesome ale,
To honour Him who by His death
Our souls from Hell did bail.

We hope ye have a fine fat goose
And puddings plump and brown,
To celebrate the birth of Him
That weareth heaven's crown.

But ere ye feast and merry make,
Good Christian people pray,

And thank the Lord that His dear Son
Was born on Christmas Day.

Then all rejoice and drink and sing;
Let mirth cast care aside.
God bless this place and grant all souls
A joyful Christmastide.

Wassail! Wassail! Wassail! Wassail! Wassail!!

Decorated Stench Pipes in Eyvesborough

The citizens of Eyvesborough are justifiably proud of their fine sewer system, designed and built during 1877-81 by the then Borough Engineer, Amos Parsifal Lunch (1835-1926). A unique feature of the system is the five "hydraulic fan stations" which use water power from the River Eyve to propel a gentle current of air through the pipes to encourage the expulsion of noxious gases. In the Eyvesborough Museum is a scribbled note written by Joseph Bazalgette to Lunch during a sanitary engineers' convention saying "I wish I'd thought of that".

Every Yuletide since Lunch died on Christmas Eve 1926, the Department of Works has decorated the town's 74 stench pipes with holly, ivy and coloured lights in tribute to the great engineer. The practice of placing lighted candles around the crown was discontinued in the 1950s, after a number of spectacular methane flares set fire to nearby buildings, including the Mayor's house and the fire station.

On Christmas morning 1938, the Rt Rev'd Edwin Dimley-Potts, Suffragan Bishop of Eyvesborough, preached a sermon on "the spirituality of stench pipes" to an enthralled congregation in Stilchester Cathedral, a feat which still stands unparalleled in the annals of theological ingenuity.

The Singing Gargoyles of Groakford

The little church of St Gertrude at Groakford, near Brobmore Regis, was founded by the monks of Scrunton Abbey c. 1210. It has a fine collection of gargoyles and grotesques, many of which survived the depredations of the Cromwellian era by being hidden in Spratte's Bog outside the village and were later reinstated in their own stalls in the chancel.

Local tradition has it that at various times during Christmas night, when they think no-one is listening, these stone monsters break forth into song. Their standard repertory consists of the mediaeval Latin text *Laudate lapes natatis rex coelum* (sic) rendered in organum. This work, hitherto unknown to scholars, was only identified in 1947 when a fragment of illuminated manuscript came to light during the removal of the pulpit for renovation.

However, the gargoyles are not lacking in versatility and since Victorian times there have been numerous well-attested accounts of their performing popular carols in close harmony. On Christmas morning 1975, the then verger swore that he had heard them singing "Mary's Boy Child" in the style of the Bay City Rollers (although some doubt was later shed on his claim by the landlady of the Gryphon's Head).

Attempts to record the gargoyles have been unsuccessful. In 2003 the Porcine Record Company, having recorded the carol service, was given permission to leave the equipment running inside the locked church overnight. Although three villagers reported hearing singing from the churchyard, the tape was blank apart from a strange sound "like water disappearing down a plug-hole". This came as no surprise to the village's senior resident, 97 year old Walter Lunch, who said "That'll be them sucking the music off the tape. They ain't mocked, y'know".

The Clabworth Carol

The gargoyles have also been known to sing this mediaeval carol, a setting of the familiar cherry tree legend.

A goodly man named Joseph, hard-working, true and staid
Betroth-ed was to Mary, a fair and comely maid.
But soon thought he some young man his bride-to-be beguiled,
For it was plain for all to see that Mary was with child.

Then in a dream an angel did speak to him and say,
"Oh Joseph, wise and kindly, put not the maid away,
For she is meek and gentle, in her there is no sin;
The Holy Spirit of the Lord doth move that maid within."

Nulla rosa castus est, nisi dominae nostrae

So Joseph, being God-fearing, did as the angel spake,
And wed the maiden Mary and took her for his make.
Then went they forth to Bethl'em, their taxes for to pay,
And came upon a cherry tree that overhung the way.

That tree was heavy laden with cherries plump and sweet.
Said Mary unto Joseph, "I fain would stop and eat.
I prithee, dearest husband, climb up the cherry tree
And pick the choicest fruit thereof and bring it down to me."

Nulla rosa castus est, nisi dominae nostrae

Then Joseph cried and curs-ed, "Yon cherry tree is tall.
My limbs are old and feeble, my stature is but small.
Let him that had his will o' thee and got thee great with child
Go do thy bidding, Mary, and fetch thee cherries wild."

Straightway the tree its branches bent down to earth so low,
And Mary plucked the tender fruit that 'twixt its leaves did grow.
Then on they went to Bethl'em and there she brought to birth
The blessed Son of God most High, the Saviour of the Earth.

Nulla rosa castus est, nisi dominae nostrae

Yuletide Hedgehogs

[From *On Stilts*, December 2006]

93 year old Mrs Florrie Wether of Inkton St Faith has been trying to encourage school children to revive the local custom of feeding hedgehogs during the winter months. At one time it was common for families to put out scraps of leftover meat at night, but children no longer dig up leatherjackets or save titbits from the Sunday roast the way they used to. The origins of the custom are unclear but it has been linked with the Blessed Witta, the revered 10th century mystic, who is known to have been fond of hedgehogs and often referred to them in his teachings.

From the 18th century onwards it became customary to give hedgehogs a special treat on Christmas Day: pieces of the crisp fat skin from the goose and "jog pies" – tiny pasties filled with worms and dried fruits enriched with spices and brandy. On Boxing Day it was not uncommon to find the creatures curled up in the coal shed, sleeping off the previous night's excesses.

Mrs Wether recalls that, as a young girl, she used to worry that the somnolent hedgehogs might be an easy prey for gypsies, who regard the animals baked in clay as a delicacy, but her grandmother reassured her that they were superstitious people and would never touch a "yuletide hog". Interestingly, the parish registers of Witterspool record that on Holy Innocents' Day in 1827 "a tinker of no fixed abode died at Snetham Green in this parish, after eating a baked hedgehog".

Listen people good and true.
Tidings rare do we bring to you.
Christian folk rejoice this day.
Christus natus hodie.

Tis the time that we all should sing,
Blow the organ and tune the string.
Go to church and thankful pray.
Solis ortus cardine.

Softly breathe with the sighing flute,
Gently finger the tender lute.
God as man to earth is come.
O magnum mysterium.

Noble sage and sweet buffoon
Praise the Lord with the great bassoon.
Sound the strain abroad and far.
In excelsis gloria.

The village of Repstock, nestling in the shelter of the North Drones, is mainly known for its crumbly, tangy, white cheese but, like nearby Flockshaw, it has a fine tradition of carol singing. The Waits leave the Dairy at sunset on Christmas Eve to sing themselves hoarse around the village and neighbouring farms, returning late to partake of mulled ale, port, venison sausages and fruit cake with cheese. Midnight is greeted with a cacophonous fanfare on the bassoons.

At Christmastide, a large ivy-clad stone is brought into the Dairy to ensure the superior quality of next year's cheese. Rat droppings are also considered a favourable omen.

The Miraculous Frying Pan of Everbone

Visitors to the church of St Audrey, Everbone, are often surprised to see an old black frying pan in the chancel.

The story begins in 1742 when the old church of St Decimus on the other side of the village was deconsecrated and a notorious felon and blasphemer, Jacob Bezzle, buried in its churchyard. He was soon joined by the evil "Warlock of Domewell", whose charred corpse had hung in a rusting gibbet at the crossroads on the boundaries of Everbone, Domewell and Britlam for almost 50 years. This provoked outrage among the villagers, many of whom attempted to dig up the bones of their ancestors and move them to the new churchyard.

The Bishop of Stilchester sought to quell this unseemly behaviour and promptly forbade the use of spades, shovels and mattocks within the parish bounds. But on Christmas Eve a widow, Mehetabel Grout, managed to exhume her late husband using only her trusty skillet and working by candlelight. Eventually the Bishop relented and gave special dispensation for the "mass re-interment of the mortal remains of the righteous of Everbone".

When Mrs Grout passed away in 1757 the frying pan was brought into the church, where it has remained ever since. And it has long been believed to possess miraculous powers, particularly at Christmastide. It is said to cure agues and chilblains and heal burns sustained in the course of culinary endeavour. Contact with a new pan is thought to endow the latter with non-stick properties and an inability to burn the bacon, so local people tend to buy new cookware during Advent and bring it to the old pan for a "blessing" on Christmas Eve.

Having heard the tale, the visitor may enquire why such an historic artefact is not kept under lock and key? The last time someone attempted to remove it from the church, back in 1911, the frying pan grew warm in his hands as he approached the door and became red hot before he even reached the lych gate, causing him to drop it forthwith. The hapless thief was apprehended shortly afterwards, trying to cool his blistered hands in the Ever Brook.

Should you be in the Three Cymbals at Trubmarsh at Christmastide, you may witness the spectacle of drinkers precariously balancing their pints on old wooden tables that have only three legs where they were clearly intended to have four.

The tiny village lies north of Gruntlington, the only place where the Temperance movement gained a foothold – nay, a toehold – in the county. In the early hours of Christmas Eve 1929 a local evangelical preacher, the Rev'd Amos Pilchard, known for his vehement condemnation of the demon drink, broke into the pub and sawed a leg off each table "to confound the spawn of Satan". When the customers arrived later they simply propped up the unstable tables with hands, knees or beer bellies and carried on drinking – and not a drop of ale was spilled. The vicar called it "a true miracle, the like of which that ranting dissenter will not comprehend, since he denies our Lord's first and great wonder wrought at Cana of Galilee."

By the time the brewery got around to replacing the tables the regulars had become highly adept at the balancing act and were reluctant to abandon the practice, even to the extent of deliberately mutilating the new furniture. Most of that resourceful band of topers have long since passed on, save Fred Pencil, at the time of writing in his 101st year. But the old tables are still brought out from Christmas Eve to the Third Sunday in Epiphany. As like as not you will find old Fred, casually maintaining the equilibrium of the table with his elbow while enjoying a pint and a joke with young Jason Pilchard, the great-grandson of the preacher.

Adam's Tree

This carol was written and set to an old Hazedale folk tune by Rev'd Benjamin Rhodes. The name may belong to an earlier set of words or it may be a reference to the old gallows at Ryming Cross, commonly known as "Adam's Tree".

Of hearthside and company I late took my leave
To walk o'er the dales on a clear frosty eve.
Deep snow in the gullies had muffled the rill,
And sheep in the heather knelt silent and still.
Silent, silent, silent and still.

I gazed at the stars with their cold crystal fire,
And mused how a star did the Wise Men inspire
To honour a King with their gifts of fine gold,
While bitter sweet spices his passion foretold.
Passion, passion, passion foretold.

I paused in my wandering while clouds hid the moon,
And leaned on a cow byre of timber rough hewn.
'Twas sturdy but draughty and grown o'er with thorn,
And in such a place the Lord Jesus was born.
Jesus, Jesus, Jesus was born.

I passed by th'old gibbet all covered in snow,
Its broken arm pointing the way I should go.
I thought on God's mercy to all men and me,
And how our dear Saviour was hung on the tree.
Saviour, Saviour, hung on the tree.

And though there was naught but the moon to give light,
It seemed that the skies grew uncommonly bright,
And, though 'twere some miles from tower or spire,
Methought I heard voices a-singing in choir:
"In Excelsis Gloria!".

While Stiltshire folk are generally God-fearing, they are not above embellishing the Christmas story in their own image. The most bizarre idea to have gained credence is the suggestion that the Magi may have been of extra-terrestrial origin.

The 19th century academic Jeromey Flanhead made an extensive study of the diaries of the mad ninth Duke of Stiltshire, written nearly two centuries earlier while the latter was imprisoned for heresy. The diaries consist mainly of dialogue between de Pailey and his celestial mentor Morfark, described as a greenish-grey humanoid about three feet tall, and there are occasional references to two companions of Morfark named Prennix and Eeybalborp. These aliens clearly belonged to a race capable of extreme longevity and were alleged to have visited Earth several times over the centuries. Flanhead became convinced that they had made one such visit at the time of the Nativity and that the Star of Bethlehem was a navigational beacon used to guide their spacecraft.

While most of Flanhead's theories have been dismissed as the ravings of an alcoholic fantasist, this one has a habit of resurfacing from time to time. In 2006 a Stilhaven Sunday school teacher was censured for dressing the Kings in clingfilm and grey, almond-eyed masks. Some years earlier the choir of St Leonard's, Shrokeby, debated the casting of "We Three Kings" at some length, deciding eventually that Morfark must be the baritone, Prennix the tenor and Eeybalborp the bass.

The Bells of Grencham

The pretty little bells of Grencham, how sweetly they ring round,
Across the woods and dells from Grencham. Mayst hear the joyful sound?
O'er meadows white and hoary they peal this Christmas morn,
To tell the world the wondrous story of Christ our blessed Saviour born.

The sturdy little bells of Grencham, they ring their changes true,
That everyone who dwells in Grencham might hear the tidings new.
They tell of sins forgiven, of innocence restored,
Of Satan and his host down-driven, when Jesus Christ shall reign as Lord.

Grencham is a small village about eight miles north-east of Brobmore Regis. This charming carol was written in 1934 by the vicar's wife, Emily Placard, and published in the Brobmore Regis Gazette in December of that year. The following week an anonymous piece of doggerel appeared in the letters column:

"Those wretched little bells of Grencham, how miserable they sound,
May heaven's almighty thunder quench 'em and may the Lord confound
The ringers who me anger, they are an artless bunch.
How dare they with their dreadful clangour disturb again my Christmas lunch?"

This in turn provoked a flurry of correspondence with one parishioner even daring to suggest that the author of the anonymous riposte was none other than the vicar himself, who was well known not to share his wife's delight in things campanological.

A highlight of the Stiltshire sporting calendar is the Christmas Pudding Olympics, held every Boxing Day at Fiddler's Field outside the village of Smitley. In their present form the games date from 1892, although they continue a much older tradition.

Among the athletic events are the Uphill Roll, where contestants have to propel a pudding along a steep, meandering 440 yard course using an implement like a hockey stick, the Pudding Put (like shot put), the High Toss and the Pyramid Jump, which involves leaping over a gradually increasing pyramid of puddings (obviously the difficulty increases exponentially as each successive layer adds both height and width). In 2003, having dominated the junior event for several years, local girl Sally Greengage, then 17, cleared an incredible 11 stack (286 puddings), breaking the previous record of a 9 stack (165) established by Major Horatio Pillion in 1936. For practical reasons all these events use special "racing puddings" made from stale breadcrumbs and dried fruit bonded with resin.

Real Christmas puddings, albeit made to a strict recipe, are used in the Henry Beef Challenge for the most 2lb puddings eaten at one sitting. The event is named after the legendary Stiltshire trencherman who, while an undergraduate at Old College, allegedly consumed 16 puddings in 1797, the same year in which he won the University Ale and Fig Contest, both feats being still unrivalled. In 2004, 13 year old Gregory Bread managed 11½ puddings, beating not only the junior record but also the official (i.e. since 1892) adult record. The speed eating event or Single Pudding Gobble was dropped in the 1950s after too many competitors complained of indigestion but later reinstated. An unfortunate incident occurred in 2001 when several competitors were inadvertently served uncured racing puddings; two were taken ill, although the winner Sumo Toriyaki claimed to prefer the texture and had to be threatened with disqualification when he asked for one the following year.

The only team event, the Flaming Pudding Relay, has been dominated since the 1970s by the Brobmore Regis Constabulary and the Stiltshire Fire Brigade (Stilhaven Division), with an exciting "photo finish" almost guaranteed and occasional also-rans like the Crachelton District Scoutmasters lagging up to half a minute behind. A promising challenge by the young employees of Aliment's Brewery was thwarted when their pudding went out.

The picture depicts a batch of racing puddings curing on Boxing morning 2010, watched over by Fred and Bert, a pair of angelic but slightly spooky Victorian funerary statues. Believed to have been stolen from Grencham churchyard in the late 19th century and never returned, they have stood in Fiddler's Field for as long as anyone can remember and are frequently offered libations of rum and mince pies by hopeful contestants.

A Lullaby of Railway

Stiltshire folk are noted for their slightly off-beat take on the Nativity, whether it be pigs worshipping at the manger or sackcloth camels pursuing a turnip-lantern star, and the carol "The Holy Virgin sweetly hummed" is no exception, its wistful melody underpinned not by the customary "lully-lullay" but by a gently rising and falling "nn-nnn nn-nnn, nn-nnn nn-nnn".

On the Saturday before Christmas in 1879 the Very Rev'd Gerald Greengage, Dean of Stilchester, was due to officiate at the wedding of his goddaughter, Mehetabel, whose father, Canon Thurleigh Kettle, was an old friend from college days and currently Rector of Eyvesborough. As the Stiltshire Railway Company had recently opened the branch line to Eyvesborough the Dean decided to take the 11.15 from Stilchester Central. His dear wife Emily was indisposed with a sprained ankle, otherwise things might have turned out rather differently.

As the train chugged through Dimley Vale, the cleric became quite mesmerised by the sound of the wheels passing over the gaps in the rails and an image began to form in his mind of the Virgin humming a cradle song to the infant Jesus. On arrival at Eyvesborough, he had quite forgotten the purpose of his visit and remained on the train in order to continue drawing inspiration from its sounds. By the time it reached Kings Pebberworth on its second return trip to Stilchester the carol was composed and the Dean had fallen asleep.

Upon arriving at Eyvesborough for the third time he was rudely awoken by a porter. By then he was three hours late and arrived at the church just in time to find the Verger locking up. They had waited for over an hour and a half but, with the bride in tears and the congregation shivering in the chill December air (there being no central heating in churches in those days), the Rector had eventually donned his robes and performed the ceremony himself.

Fortunately, Prudence Swallow of the local brewery had been in church and hastily arranged for a couple of firkins of her best old ale to be decanted into large jugs and rushed to the church hall to warm the freezing guests as they arrived for the reception. Mellowed by the ale and learning the cause of his lateness, the bride was able to forgive her godfather. Indeed Mehetabel, a mezzo-soprano of no mean ability, was deeply moved by the carol and it was she who gave its first public performance in Stilchester Cathedral the following year.

Edible Crib Figures

"Mummy, Mummy, Rex has eaten Melchior!"

Whilst Stiltshire families generally keep their Christmas Crib out of reach of small children and dogs, it is not uncommon around Boxing Day to discover a headless magus or an ox with teeth marks in its rump. This is because there is a tradition of using edible figures for the peripheral characters in the tableau (shepherds, wise men, angels, oxen, asses and pigs). The central figures are normally wooden or ceramic though; there is a widespread feeling that it would be somewhat akin to blasphemy to eat the Baby Jesus* or the Virgin Mary. Whether Joseph should be edible or not has long been a matter of debate.

Most of these consumable crib sets are manufactured by Gruntlington Sugarsmiths, the firm renowned for Dr John's Chalky Mints, Clove Snakes and Chorister's Choice, but a more exclusive version can be obtained from Halbard and Poussin of Brobmore Regis (available by mail order or from Brogue's Department Store). Cognoscenti generally agree that King Balthazar, made from 88% Madagascan dark chocolate, is the most esculent.

* Although the Archdeacon of Plean, the Ven. Dr Hedley Pencil, has argued that administering chocolate babes in swaddling clothes at the Eucharist would be theologically sound and powerfully illustrate the inexorable link between the Nativity and the Passion.

Uproost ye fro' ye'r drusky sleep
And bratly fro' ye'r truckle leap.
The sprattled cock his chaunt ha' sorn,
"Awek, brave souls, 'tis Christmas morn".

The grumbent clouds ha' sne'en a' night
And sproon the fales wi' greckit white.
The eldern tree, though naggled crone,
Doth wear a trinkled bridal gown.

Arise and bake ye'r Christmas breel.
Away to church and meekly kneel;
To God our Heavenly Father pray.
Then celebrate this gladsome day.

This carol is sung at Goadinger and Hazzock early on Christmas morning. Some of the more obscure words in the Hazedale dialect are explained below:

drusky - drowsy; *bratly* - in a spritely manner; *sprattled* - speckled; *sorn* - sung; *grumbent* - dark and lowering; *sne'en* - snowed; *sproon* - strewn, sprinkled; *fales* - hillsides; *greckit* - coat or blanket; *naggled* - gnarled, haggard; *trinkled* - sparkling; *breel* - a savoury lardy-cake stuffed with pork and cheese, eaten with plum jam for breakfast on Christmas morning.

The Strange Tale of the Archdeacon's Teeth

It was Christmas Eve 1922. The Archdeacon of Spruntley, the Venerable Cecil Spiggott, awoke from his evening nap to discover that his false teeth were not on the arm of his chair where he was quite sure he had left them. He was alone in the house. His wife had been at the parish hall all evening preparing supper for the poor widows from the alms-houses and his daughter, he assumed, was with her. The maid had left at four o'clock to spend Christmas with her family in Obervole. Frantically he searched his study, the bedroom, bathroom and scullery but all to no avail.

The time was fast approaching when he should be celebrating Midnight Mass at St Aldhelm's. Embarrassed, he donned his hat and coat and made his way thither. It was only as the crucifer began to lead the procession into the nave that his daughter appeared, breathless, and thrust something into his hand with the words "I think you might need these, Daddy".

It later transpired that she had been serving plates of roast pork to the poor widows and noticed that they seemed somewhat reluctant to tackle the crackling. Upon enquiry she learned that they possessed not a single tooth between them. Now it was quite inconceivable to the child that anyone should have to sit before a dish of the finest Prumeford Russet flesh and be unable to savour the best part of it, so she swiftly devised a plan and soon the grateful crones were enabled to enjoy their crackling, albeit in relays.

Come the New Year, the Archdeacon found it necessary to obtain a new set of dentures, for the old ones never quite fitted properly after that. But at least he was able to sit down to his Christmas goose content in the knowledge that he – or at least his teeth – may have entertained angels unawares.

The Spiggott family still live in the same house in Spruntley. In 1987 the old dentures unexpectedly came to light at the back of a cupboard, since when, every Christmas Eve, they are placed on the arm of the "venerable chair" before being taken up in the offertory procession at St Aldhelm's.

The Goose-eating Fairy of Mythern

On Christmas morning in the church hall at Mythern there are always two plump geese roasting in the ancient gas oven. There are no vegetables or puddings; this act of charity is not to feed the homeless, for there are none in Mythern these days, but to compensate any family whose festive fowl may have been spirited away by a mischievous fairy.

Nearly every Christmas since about 1690 there has been at least one report of a goose stolen from the kitchen table while the cook's back was turned or even snatched from the oven. Walkers on Boxing Day morning often find a heap of bones at the bottom of Sorrel Lane.

To call the thief a fairy is perhaps a misnomer. On the rare occasions when the culprit has been glimpsed scurrying down the garden path with its prize held aloft, reports of its appearance differ widely. The Rev'd Samuel Plank in 1875 described it thus: "a rotund, hairy creature, not much above two feet tall, with stubby legs, a florid complexion and a wide mouth". Others however have recalled the delicate features more commonly attributed to the fairy race or perhaps something more akin to an orc or goblin.

While one or two geese normally go missing the record is six. A few people have attempted to thwart the fairy by buying a turkey (it appears to disdain the American interloper) but this break with tradition is generally frowned upon. One recent Christmas the two geese in the church hall disappeared but it didn't matter because no home in the village was affected. The following year when, at the suggestion of the Curate, the hall was deliberately left unattended, both geese were untouched but the Pencil family next door lost theirs.

Sceptics have sometimes drawn attention to the population of healthy, well-fed foxes in the area but the good folk of Mythern will have none of it: "Foxes running on their hind legs and opening oven doors? Pah!"

[In recent times the fairy seems to have acquired a taste for Stanley Carnage's Bacon Scones — three dozen were stolen from the Organist's Arms last Christmas Eve.]

The Star of Squbberton

Although more than 60 years have passed, many folk still remember with awe the singular events which took place in the tiny village of Squbberton on Christmas Night 1956.

The first person to notice anything untoward was Jack Shin the verger. He had cycled to the Boar's Head in Hogberrow for a couple of pints and at about a quarter to eleven was on his way to church to prepare for Midnight Mass. As he passed Hazel Farm he became aware of a minor commotion. The pigs were leaving their sties, grunting agitatedly and glancing skyward, where lowering clouds threatened to obscure the waxing gibbous moon. Thinking this a little odd, Jack made a mental note to tell farmer Blagness after the service. Meanwhile, over at Little Pudding Farm, Mrs Oyster had noticed their pigs too were getting restless.

It was about half past twelve when the congregation, led by a quartet of exuberant choirboys, emerged from church to find all the pigs in the village assembled on the glebe, squatting quietly on their haunches and looking expectantly upwards. Suddenly the clouds parted and an uncommonly bright star cast its radiance upon the animals. The three mediaeval bells in the little wooden steeple (affectionately known as "three tone deaf mice") began to chime of their own accord, swinging higher and higher until the ancient timbers shuddered and groaned alarmingly.

And then the moment had passed – the clouds reconvened, the bells ceased their clangour and the pigs trotted home to their respective farms and smallholdings, followed by their bemused owners. As they departed a light flurry of snow began to fall and by morning every tree, hedgerow and rooftop was clad in dazzling whiteness.

At Matins and in the Acorn Inn afterwards, people spoke in hushed tones of "the miracle" and wondered "Why Squbberton?" As a kind of thanksgiving the bells were rehung in a new frame. And for some years afterwards the inhabitants bought all their pork and bacon from neighbouring villages, since none could bring themselves to eat any pig which had been so spectacularly blessed.

And another thing – to this day no-one can explain how a lump of rock weighing an estimated seven tons and shaped like a Christmas pudding, complete with flames and sprig of holly, found its way into the vicarage garden that night.

Peace on Gnashing Bridge

Gnashing Bridge in Stilchester is an ancient stone walkway that spans the River Stilt in the heart of the city. Although a foot bridge, it is wide enough to accommodate the passage of a pair of horses or an hogshead of ale. Between its two arches is a rhomboidal platform surmounted by a small round tower.

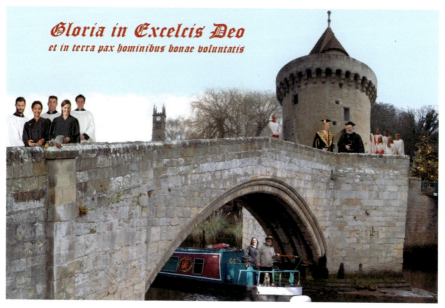

The bridge is roughly equidistant between those venerable seats of learning, St Cedd's and Old College. Consequently, it has traditionally been a favoured site for fierce debate between rival academics. Whilst these exchanges are generally amicable, they have occasionally come to blows, most tragically in 1741 when Amos Bludge, Professor of Mathematics at Old College, fell over the parapet and broke his head, whereupon his opposite number Professor Samuel Wenton fled to Stilhaven with his parrot Pythagoras to embark upon a second career as Saucy Sam the pirate.

Goodwill prevails, however, on Christmas morning, when the Masters of St Cedd's and Old College meet to take wine and exchange gifts while their respective chapel choirs sing carols, albeit antiphonally from opposite ends of the bridge. By this time the pubs are open and there is much running to and fro across the bridge with tankards of ale. The carol singing normally attracts an appreciative audience, not only of city folk but of passing boaters on the river.

Easter in Stiltshire begins at dawn as it has done for centuries with a huge bonfire at Trinkle Cross, that ancient meeting of six roads in the South Drones. From there the Paschal flame is carried to the four corners of the county.

Traditionally the flame was carried on horseback but since the 1930s the vehicles of choice have been six Rumbler *Resurrection* motorcycles built by the Gruntlington firm of George Rumble and co. These magnificent 1200cc V-twin machines were a limited edition quite unlike the company's popular 200cc *Runabout*. Although the firm ceased trading in 1964, members of the Rumble family still run a small workshop in Trubmarsh, where the nine surviving Resurrections are lovingly serviced and maintained for the benefit of their proud owners, including the Bishop of Stilchester the Rt Rev'd Spencer Kettle, a lifelong motor cycling enthusiast.

Last year the threatened rain failed to materialise and at the first glimmer of the rising sun over the hilltops the tarpaulins were removed and the bonfire of larch wood and waste paper set alight. After the initial prayers, the Bishop lit the first torch with a triumphal shout of "Christ is risen!". As the assembled congregation responded with a mighty cry of "He is risen indeed!", his son Gavin kicked the ancient motorcycle into action and the Bishop, wearing his gold cope and unique mitre-shaped crash helmet, mounted the pillion seat and the bike roared into the gloom carrying the blazing torch.

26 minutes later the Rumbler pulled up at the west door of the cathedral where the Dean was waiting to light the Paschal candle. As the procession moved into the nave and the basso profundo Quainton Rhodes began to intone the *Exultet* in the wonderful Russian-sounding setting by Dr Ashley Pencil, Gavin remounted the bike and set off on the next leg of the journey via Chaddlestead, Pyke Wilberton and Prokeworth to Stilhaven, whence the flame would be carried by boat across to St Botolph's chapel on Gryatt Island.

Meanwhile the other five riders were following their centuries old routes: Johnnie Rumble took the second and longest - westward to Spruntley and then south to Great Knorrley and Chineham Gregory and thence through the villages of Dongland to finish on the quay at Japhetstowe. The third rider set off to the north-west, to Stiltford and Everbone and then eastwards through the North Drones to Great Ryming and Cauldby; the fourth north-east to Vazeworth, down through Dimley Vale to Eyvesborough and then south to East Pawtley, Plean and Eyvemouth; the fifth southwards to Prumeford, Wizard's Alton, Jupton and Smitley, ending at Brobmore Regis; and the sixth via Kings Pebberworth and Hogberrow to Bayconhurst, Gruntlington and Apstrow. At each stop Paschal candles would be lit and the flame relayed by whatever means were available to the neighbouring villages, so that by mid-morning every church in the Diocese had received the "light of Christ".

After jubilant celebrations of the victory over sin and death, most folk naturally repair to the pubs where strong, hoppy Easter ales have been freshly tapped to replace the more subdued and astringent brews normally drunk during Lent and Holy Week. And then they will wend their way home for a celebratory dinner where, for once, roast lamb with holy rosemary is the norm rather than pork.

Harvest Festival

As a predominantly rural county, Stiltshire has every reason to celebrate Harvest Home enthusiastically, but even in the towns and cities every church holds its Harvest Festival in the traditional manner. There are no tins of beans or packets of cornflakes before the altar, but gargantuan marrows lining the aisles, apples piled high on window ledges, sheaves of corn and bunches of grapes. Most parishes hold a Harvest Lunch or Supper at which the produce is auctioned for charity or donated to local hospitals and care homes.

And naturally the breweries will have produced something special to mark the occasion.

The de Pailey Dynasty

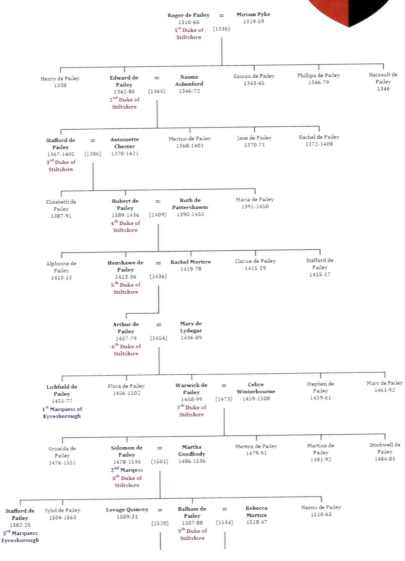

Roger de Pailey
1310-65
1st Duke of
Stiltshire
= (1336)
Miriam Pyke
1319-59

Henry de Pailey
1338

Edward de Pailey
1342-80
2nd Duke of Stiltshire
= (1365)
Naomi Ashenford
1346-72

Gascon de Pailey
1343-45

Phillipa de Pailey
1346-79

Hainault de Pailey
1346

Stafford de Pailey
1367-1405
3rd Duke of Stiltshire
= (1386)
Antoinette Chester
1370-1421

Merton de Pailey
1368-1401

Jane de Pailey
1370-71

Rachel de Pailey
1372-1408

Elizabeth de Pailey
1387-91

Hubert de Pailey
1389-1436
4th Duke of Stiltshire
= (1409)
Ruth de Pattershawm
1390-1455

Maria de Pailey
1391-1450

Alphonse de Pailey
1410-13

Henshawe de Pailey
1413-36
5th Duke of Stiltshire
= (1436)
Rachel Mortice
1419-78

Clarice de Pailey
1415-59

Stafford de Pailey
1415-17

Arthur de Pailey
1437-79
6th Duke of Stiltshire
= (1454)
Mary de Lydegar
1436-89

Lichfield de Pailey
1455-77
1st Marquess of Eyvesborough

Flora de Pailey
1456-1502

Warwick de Pailey
1458-99
7th Duke of Stiltshire
= (1473)
Celice Winterbourne
1459-1508

Stephen de Pailey
1459-61

Mary de Pailey
1461-92

Griselda de Pailey
1476-1551

Solomon de Pailey
1478-1536
2nd Marqess
8th Duke of Stiltshire
= (1501)
Martha Goodbody
1486-1536

Merton de Pailey
1479-91

Martina de Pailey
1481-92

Stockwell de Pailey
1484-85

Stafford de Pailey
1502-25
3rd Marquess Eyvesborough

Sybil de Pailey
1504-1563

Lovage Quincey
1509-31
= (1528)
Balham de Pailey
1507-88
9th Duke of Stiltshire
= (1534)
Rebecca Mortice
1518-47

Naomi de Pailey
1510-63

The de Pailey Dynasty

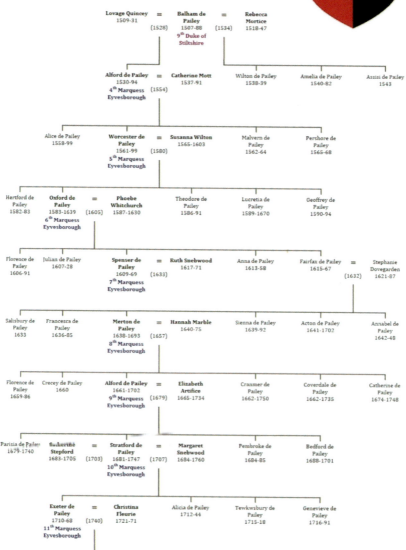

Lovage Quincey 1509-31 = Balham de Pailey 1507-88 9th Duke of Stiltshire (1528) = Rebecca Mortice 1518-47 (1534)

Alford de Pailey 1530-94 4th Marquess Eyvesborough (1554) = Catherine Mott 1537-91 | Wilton de Pailey 1538-39 | Amelia de Pailey 1540-82 | Assisi de Pailey 1543

Alice de Pailey 1558-99 | Worcester de Pailey 1561-99 5th Marquess Eyvesborough (1580) = Susanna Wilton 1565-1603 | Malvern de Pailey 1562-64 | Pershore de Pailey 1565-68

Hertford de Pailey 1582-83 | Oxford de Pailey 1583-1639 6th Marquess Eyvesborough (1605) = Phoebe Whitchurch 1587-1630 | Theodore de Pailey 1586-91 | Lucretia de Pailey 1589-1670 | Geoffrey de Pailey 1590-94

Florence de Pailey 1606-91 | Julian de Pailey 1607-28 | Spenser de Pailey 1609-69 7th Marquess Eyvesborough (1633) = Ruth Snebwood 1617-71 | Anna de Pailey 1613-58 | Fairfax de Pailey 1615-67 (1632) = Stephanie Dovegarden 1621-87

Salisbury de Pailey 1633 | Francesca de Pailey 1636-85 | Merton de Pailey 1638-1693 8th Marquess Eyvesborough (1657) = Hannah Marble 1640-75 | Sienna de Pailey 1639-92 | Acton de Pailey 1641-1702 | Annabel de Pailey 1642-48

Florence de Pailey 1659-86 | Crecey de Pailey 1660 | Alford de Pailey 1661-1702 9th Marquess Eyvesborough (1679) = Elizabeth Artifice 1665-1734 | Cranmer de Pailey 1662-1750 | Coverdale de Pailey 1662-1735 | Catherine de Pailey 1674-1748

Parisia de Pailey 1679-1740 | Katherine Stepford 1683-1705 (1703) = Stratford de Pailey 1681-1747 10th Marquess Eyvesborough (1707) = Margaret Snebwood 1684-1760 | Pembroke de Pailey 1684-85 | Bedford de Pailey 1688-1701

Exeter de Pailey 1710-68 11th Marquess Eyvesborough (1740) = Christina Fleurie 1721-71 | Alicia de Pailey 1712-44 | Tewkwsbury de Pailey 1715-18 | Genevieve de Pailey 1716-91

The de Pailey Dynasty

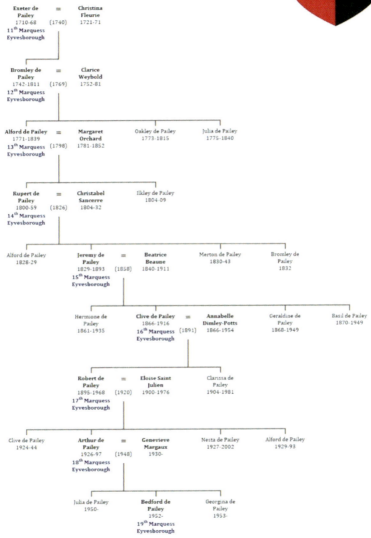

Exeter de Pailey 1710-68 = (1740) Christina Fleure 1721-71
11th Marquess Eyvesborough

Bromley de Pailey 1742-1811 = (1769) Clarice Weybold 1752-81
12th Marquess Eyvesborough

Alford de Pailey 1771-1839 = (1798) Margaret Orchard 1781-1852 — Oakley de Pailey 1773-1815 — Julia de Pailey 1775-1840
13th Marquess Eyvesborough

Rupert de Pailey 1800-59 = (1826) Christabel Sancerre 1804-32 — Ilkley de Pailey 1804-09
14th Marquess Eyvesborough

Alford de Pailey 1828-29 — Jeremy de Pailey 1829-1893 = (1858) Beatrice Beaune 1840-1911 — Merton de Pailey 1830-43 — Bromley de Pailey 1832
15th Marquess Eyvesborough

Hermione de Pailey 1861-1935 — Clive de Pailey 1866-1916 = (1891) Annabelle Dimley-Potts 1866-1954 — Geraldine de Pailey 1868-1949 — Basil de Pailey 1870-1949
16th Marquess Eyvesborough

Robert de Pailey 1895-1968 = (1920) Eloise Saint Julien 1900-1976 — Clarissa de Pailey 1904-1981
17th Marquess Eyvesborough

Clive de Pailey 1924-44 — Arthur de Pailey 1926-97 = (1948) Genevieve Margaux 1930- — Nesta de Pailey 1927-2002 — Alford de Pailey 1929-93
18th Marquess Eyvesborough

Julia de Pailey 1950- — Bedford de Pailey 1952- — Georgina de Pailey 1953-
19th Marquess Eyvesborough

Stiltshire - North West

Miles 0 1 2 3 4 5

Henbrowe
Britlam
Everbone
Crobarge
Strupton
R Stilt
Domewell
Jearing St Thomas
Wittering Reed
R Umple
Stiltford
Jearing All Saints
Stiltford & Fletley
Eyvesborough Canal
Narkington
Umplington
Quisham
Tossfield
Growell
Dower Hill
Hornbower
Cruftmere
Spruntley
R Sprunt
Dafferd Downs
Poborough
Long Dafferd
Wittenspool Hill
Oxbake Woods
Great Knorrley
Inkton St Ann
West Knorrley
Epfield
Oxbake
Inkton St Faith
Knorrley Forest
Stilchester
Obervole
Chaddlestead
Shuckerton
R Vole
Newton St Robin
Breen
Aggerby
Breen Hill
Over Bolsacre
Clamburton
Gristlecombe
Snibling Magna
Nether Bolsacre
Silent Bolsacre
Snibling Parva
Ruckworth
Smoatham

▬▬ Major road	✝ Church	🏠 Brewery
▬▬ Minor road	✝ Cathedral	✗ Battlefield
▬▬ Railway (station)	✝ Abbey/Priory	✦ Lighthouse
▬▬ Canal (lock)	▥ Castle	⊥ Folly/Obelisk
▬▬ Footway	▥ Stately home	⊛ Quarry

✈ Airfield

Stiltshire - North East

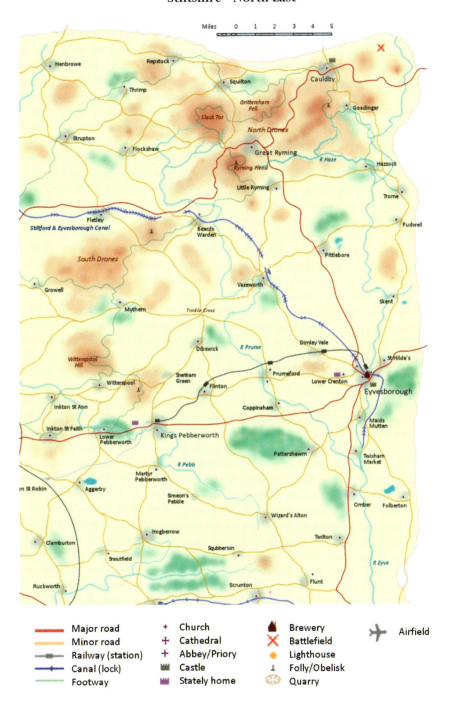

Stiltshire - South West (Dongland)

Obervole

Skittering

Debble

Hippleton Grace

Hippleton Mercy

R Fodder

Greyt Mong

Chineham Saul

Poke Bunting

Oyker

Archers Broat

Eyt Mongs

West Broat

Brinceton

Smolder

Cowpole

Broatlet

Bishops Broat

R Twom

Yurch

Flover

Great Broat

Tw...

Tworpsbridge

R Hoke

St Orry's

Widdlestone

Fruspool

Japhetstow

Saltacle

Blefton

St Togan

Devil's Buttocks

Gostable

St Enoch

Miles 0 1 2 3 4 5

▬▬ Major road	✛ Church	🍺 Brewery	✈ Airfield
▬▬ Minor road	✚ Cathedral	✖ Battlefield	
▬▬ Railway (station)	✛ Abbey/Priory	☀ Lighthouse	
▬▬ Canal (lock)	⛫ Castle	⊥ Folly/Obelisk	
▬▬ Footway	⬛ Stately home	✺ Quarry	

174

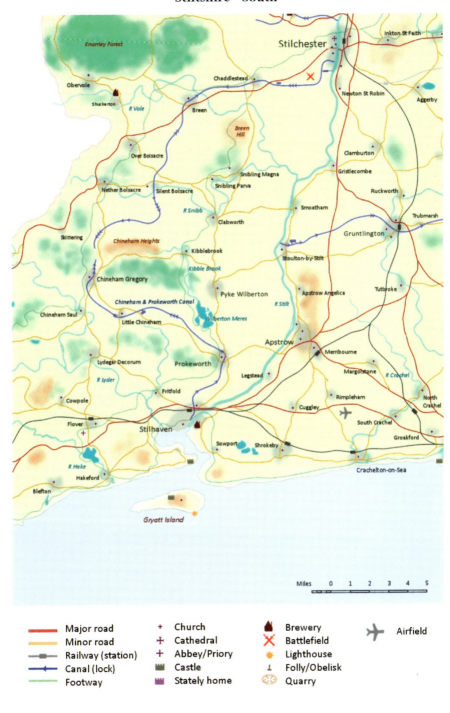

| | Miles | 0 | 1 | 2 | 3 | 4 | 5 |

━━━ Major road	+ Church
━━━ Minor road	✚ Cathedral
━━━ Railway (station)	✠ Abbey/Priory
━━━ Canal (lock)	♨ Castle
━━━ Footway	♨ Stately home

🔥 Brewery	✈ Airfield
✗ Battlefield	
☀ Lighthouse	
⊥ Folly/Obelisk	
⊛ Quarry	

Stiltshire - South East

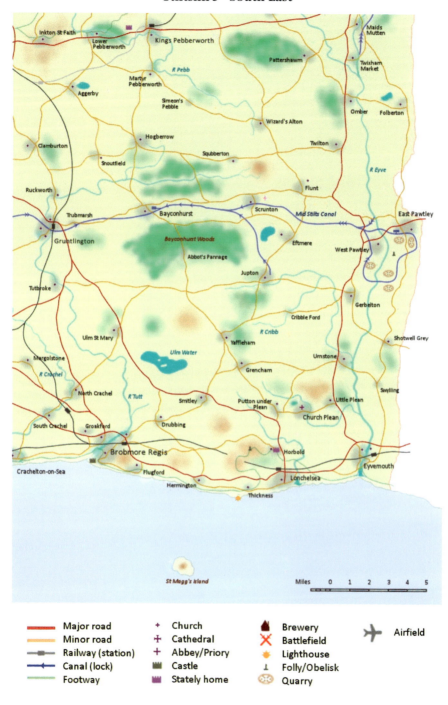

The City of Stilchester

to Stiltford

to Oxbake & Spruntley

R Stilt

Water Meadows

to the Pebberworths & Eyvesborough

to Chaddlestead & the Bolsacres

Erasmus Park

to Aggerby

Canal

R Celly

to Gruntlington & Apstrow

| 0 | ½ | 1 mile |

Main road	Railway	Public house
Secondary road	(disused)	Church
Minor road	Tramway	Historic building
Footway	Canal	Castle/Fort

The City of Stilchester

Key to map:

1	Dean's Bridge	23	St Jude's Church
2	Church of St Botolph without Norgate	24	Ezra Rhodes Museum of Stiltshire Lore
3	Circus Minimus	25	Civic Centre
4	Old Market Cross	26	Bishop's Bridge
5	Verger's Tunnel	27	St Radegund's Church
6	Observatory	28	Gnashing Bridge
7	Bishop and Sunset inn	29	St Cedd's College (UoS)
8	Cathedral of St Cedd and the Holy Rood	30	Site of Stilchester West Station
9	St Orry's Church	31	Quiritic Almshouses
10	Sievewright's Hall	32	St Ewburga's Chapel
11	St Magnus' Church	33	Municipal Baths
12	St Anthony's Church	34	New Market
13	Museum of Porcine Husbandry	35	Church of All Souls, Sowgate
14	Stilchester Central Station	36	St Thomas' Church
15	Tram Depot	37	Stangley Bridge
16	St Raphael's Hospital	38	Stangley Hall (UoS)
17	Hymnodical Library	39	St Maurice's Church
18	St Candida's Church	40	Strenshaw Galleries
19	Old Bridge	41	Opera House
20	Old College (University of Stilchester)	42	St Xavier's Church
21	Columbine Theatre	43	Stilchester Academy
22	St Agnes' Church	44	Marina

Acknowledgements

to Gill: for proof-reading and for tolerating and encouraging my eccentricities

to Ben: for creating additional characters, story-lines and music

to my ancestors: for making me the kind of person who would create an imaginary county

and to my friends who have enjoyed the Stiltshire Christmas cards and thereby inadvertently encouraged me to publish the Chronicles

Index

Printed in Poland
by Amazon Fulfillment
Poland Sp. z o.o., Wrocław